—A Novel—

Lynn Carr

Copyright © 2000 by Lynn Carr
All rights reserved.

No part of this book may be reproduced in any form whatsoever, whether by graphic, visual, electronic, filming, microfilming, tape recording, or any other means, without written permission of the author, except in the case of brief passages embodied in critical reviews and articles where the author, title and ISBN are mentioned.

This book is not an official publication of The Church of Jesus Christ of Latter-day Saints. All opinions expressed herein are the author's and are not necessarily those of the publisher or of The Church of Jesus Christ of Latter-day Saints.

Published and Distributed by:

Granite Publishing and Distribution, L.L.C.
868 North 1430 West • Orem, UT 84057
(801) 229-9023 • Toll Free (800) 574-5779
FAX (801) 229-1924

Production by Sunrise Publishing, Orem, Utah
ISBN: 1-930980-37-X
Library of Congress Control Number: 2001092135

I dedicate this novel to three people who have been responsible for its success: to Hank, my mentor, to Mary for her diligence and suggestions, and to Nora for not allowing me to give up.

Acknowledgments

Writing a novel takes a great deal of research and is essential to its success, but coming up with an exciting plot, creating the characters, knowing how to show and not tell and keeping the reader's attention—among other secrets of the trade—are all equally important. As a published writer of non-fiction and educational books and articles, I thought switching to fiction would be simple: it was not.

First, I wish to thank my mentor, Hank Searls, for 52 single spaced pages of criticism on my first try, even though after reading them I felt like jumping off a cliff. But he said I had potential and I should not give up. I started again and rewrote the entire manuscript.

With my second try, research became fundamental and took almost as much time as writing the novel. I began at the Main Precinct of the Portland Police Bureau. Sincere gratitude goes to everyone there: I was welcomed warmly and my questions were answered willingly as I filled my notebook with valuable information. I am especially indebted to Mary A. Brandon, Senior Criminalist, who took time to have lunch with me. After I completed the manuscript, she read every page to check for accuracy and realism.

Gratitude goes to specialists at the crime lab and to Terry and Julia who explained DNA, to Jim Bixby, Criminalist, regarding tire impressions, to the person in the records division and to the policeman who gave me a tour of the building from the exercise room to the Chief's office on the 13th floor. He even allowed me to handle a Glock, the weapon used by the officers, and he explained its composition.

Further gratitude goes to the Federal Bureau of Investigation for statistics regarding kidnappings, to Larry Jamison, a paramedic at Seaside, and to numerous other individuals who contributed to this novel.

But special thanks goes Nora who would not allow me to give up. She, too, read *Premonition* in its entirety and made many helpful suggestions.

Prologue

The scream pierced the early morning silence like the shriek of an angry leopard. He bolted upright in his bed, reached for his gun and looked around the room. No one was there. Then he realized: the cry had come from his own throat. No, from deep within his body. From memories.

He waited and listened for running footsteps in the hall. No one came. Exhausted, he fell back and began to shake. The sheets were damp from perspiration and the room was cold. He pulled himself from the bed, touched the thermostat and walked to the window. As he stood there listening to the familiar click of the radiator, he watched the crimson dawn spill across the Willamette.

It would be his first day back after a week at the beach. He wasn't ready to work; he wanted to go back to clam digging and surfing and climbing the wet rocks. Back to feeding the seagulls. He didn't want to reopen the case, to remember what had happened that night eleven years ago.

But Sam had come home. She said she knew her sister was still alive. Maybe she'd found new evidence; maybe she was right.

Reluctantly, he pulled himself from the window and headed for the shower. O'Malley would be calling soon. He'd ask if he had remembered to bring seashells for his granddaughter. It would be his excuse for finding out if Gordon had come back— or if he had decided to turn in his badge, buy a sloop and head on down the coast. Maybe he would someday; maybe he would. For now, he had a long and boring day ahead, catching up on paperwork and being briefed on another dull case he knew O'Malley would assign him.

And tonight he would be with Samantha for the first time in five years.

He dressed, removed a shoulder holster from the drawer where it had lain for over a week and strapped it to his body. He tucked his Smith & Wesson snub-nose revolver into the ankle holster that had become as much a routine part of his dress as the watch Sam had given him years ago. He wondered why he'd kept up the ritual: he hadn't used it in months. He checked his Glock to see that it was loaded, shoved it into the shoulder holster and put the seashells in his pocket.

As he closed the door after leaving his apartment, he heard the phone ring: it would be O'Malley. He decided not to go back. *Let him sweat,* he thought as he ambled down two flights of stairs. *The chief is an old woman; he needs to retire.*

But in his heart, he knew it wouldn't be the same without O'Malley there. Maybe the chief was his reason for coming back.

One

The day was long and boring, just as he predicted it would be. He gave the shells to O'Malley and enjoyed the expression on his face when he told him he had bought a sloop. He'd admit the truth someday—after the chief fretted awhile.

It was a quarter to four when he opened the lower, right drawer of his desk and looked down at the small, furry teddy bear—it had lain there for eleven years. It was dirty and matted and had one missing eye. He didn't know why he kept it; he should have returned it to the Ballards years ago. Perhaps he wanted it as a reminder of the promise he made to Samantha—the promise he never kept.

He spent six years working on the case, trying to find Sam's kidnapped sister. In time, he was convinced she was dead although it was never proven: there was never a corpus delicti. Except for the bicycle, a black shoe was the only positive evidence found. There were no tire tracks, no buttons, no strands of hair and no signs of struggle—not even a witness to the crime.

He pulled the teddy bear from its resting place, turned it over and over in his hands and felt the pangs of regret well up inside him once again. Regret? Or was it guilt?

He decided to go home early and shower again before picking up Sam. Without motive, he pushed the little bear into his coat pocket and left.

He paused for a moment on the back steps of the precinct and watched the people in the park across the street. Traffic was beginning to show signs of the late afternoon rush hour, and somewhere out on the Willamette a freighter sounded its warning horn as it moved slowly towards the Columbia.

Too hot for October, he thought as he ambled down the familiar steps without looking down. He knew them well. He wondered how many times he had used them in the twelve years he was a detective for the city of Portland, Oregon.

He wasn't a big man, but his body was hard and lean, and on better days he moved with the ease of a panther. His hair—bushy, but neatly trimmed—was the color of a lion and his eyes were deep blue-green. The determination of his square-cut jaw was a striking contrast to the softening of the dimple in his chin. His name was Wesley Gordon.

He crossed the street and entered the South parking lot, then remembered he'd been lucky: a space had been open in front of the building when he arrived that morning.

His car was stifling hot. He started the engine, rolled down the windows and flicked on the air conditioner. As he pulled away from the curb and rolled the windows up again, he decided to go back to the scene of the crime before going home. There was still time.

Gordon turned into the park, stopped the car and got out. He tried to recall the facts. Lazily, he walked across the lawn to the clump of trees where the bicycle had been found. He pulled the teddy bear from his pocket and stared at it as if he were expecting it to tell him something—to reveal some new piece of evidence they had missed. He sat down at the picnic table, the same one that had been there that night. It was old and grimy now and etched with love notes and initials. As his finger traced a heart pierced by an arrow, the events of that night eleven years ago returned. He had tried to erase it from his memory, but it all came too easily, as if it had been just yesterday.

଼ଷ   ଽ

"Gordon, they need a detective up in the West hills. Wanna take it?"

It had been a long and hectic day at the precinct and Detective Wesley Gordon wanted to go home before it started raining. He looked at his watch; it was 11:45 PM. *Oh, what the heck*, he thought as he turned and took the slip of paper from the stretched out hand. Later, he wished he hadn't.

It was the address of James Ballard, a prominent Portland citizen and president of a local savings and loan, whose thirteen-year-old daughter had just been kidnapped.

Gordon drove up the crooked streets of the West hills to the Ballard home and was met at the door by Officer Ratcliff. He stepped into the entry and onto a marble floor that looked as if it had just been polished by a compulsive housemaid. As the officer was introducing him to Ballard, a woman, about forty—small in stature and with delicate features—descended a massive, circular stairway. She had been crying, but the tears had not washed away her simple beauty. Ballard introduced her as his wife Carla and led them into the living room.

James Ballard was a tall, slender man with a neatly trimmed mustache that matched his chocolate-brown hair. His artificial composure echoed in the handshake he gave Ballard as he introduced himself for the second time. Beckoning to two velvet chairs, he offered them a seat. He and his wife sat on the sofa.

Gordon asked the questions while the officer took notes. "What makes you think your daughter was kidnapped?"

"I got a phone call about eight-thirty," replied the banker.

"Man or woman?"

"It sounded like a man's voice."

"Tell me exactly what he said," ordered Gordon.

"He said he had my daughter and that I was to have a hundred-thousand in cash ready to turn over to him by ten o'clock. He said..." Ballard's voice broke as he reached for his wife's hand. "He said we would never see her again if I called the police or if I didn't have the money by ten. Then he hung up."

Gordon regretted he'd taken the case. Clasping his hands together, he leaned forward, supported his arms on his knees and looked down at the rich carpet. This would be his first kidnap case since he'd made detective, and he felt inadequate. "What did you do then?" he asked.

"I got the money..."

Gordon sat upright. "A hundred thou is a lot of cash. Where'd you get it?"

"From the vault at the bank."

"At eight-thirty at night?" The detective squinted dubiously. Getting into a bank vault after the time lock had been set was not that easy, even for the bank's president.

Ballard detected Gordon's incertitude and explained. "I'm not just president, I'm half-owner of the bank. I hold the entire combination to the lock. My associates and I agreed to that long ago."

That was only half an explanation. Gordon wanted more. "But the time lock. You would have set off the alarm."

"No," came Ballard's response. "I never set it before I left. Normally, I set the lock before I leave."

"You didn't set it? Why not?"

Ballard hesitated, and then went on. "There's something I haven't told you." He looked at his wife who seemed to be in another world. "I got a call at the bank just before six—the same voice that called later. He told me not to set the time lock tonight."

"And you complied? Just like that!"

"He said I would know why later, and if I valued my..." he paused, "...if I valued my family, I wouldn't tell anyone about the call."

"Who knows you hold the entire combination?"

"No one, except my associates and our manager!"

Ballard's story disturbed the detective, but not wanting to delay the investigation, Gordon moved on while the officer scribbled nervously, trying to get it all down.

"Okay," he said, "let's go on. So you left the time lock off, came home, and the second call about your daughter and the ransom came through at eight-thirty. Then what?"

"Like I said, I went to the bank and got the money." Ballard jumped to his feet. "Wait a minute. It's not what you think! I left a note in the vault to replace it. It was my promise to return the money as soon as I could cash in a CD. I intend to take care of the details tomorrow morning!"

The explanation satisfied the detective—for now. He motioned for Ballard to calm himself and be seated. More important was the fact that a child was in the hands of a kidnapper and every moment was precious. The matter of how Ballard got the money could be handled later. "Okay, okay," he said. "Let's get on with the story."

Ballard took his wife's hand into his again and continued.

"What did you do then?" Gordon asked.

"Like I said, I went to the bank and took the money from the vault, then I came back to the house and waited."

"Go on," urged the detective.

"He called right after ten. He told me to put the money in a brown paper bag and drive to the alley behind McKinley's Market where I was to drop it in a garbage can. He said I could pick up my daughter ten minutes later in back of Wilson Elementary."

"So you dropped the money, then..." Gordon's attention was distracted by movement in the hall. He glanced toward the door and saw a young girl clinging to its edge. Ballard invited her in and she ran and sat beside her mother.

She was clad in a pink nightgown that she tucked around her legs as she pulled her knees to her chest. She had long, golden curls and tear-stained, peach-colored skin that reminded him of a porcelain doll he had once seen in a toy store. Ballard said her name was Samantha and that she and Cindy were identical twins.

Gordon stared at her for a moment and then went on with the questions. "What time did you arrive at the school?"

"About ten-thirty-five. But she wasn't there. I waited for twenty minutes or so, then called out for her. After driving around the schoolyard, I realized what a sucker I'd been and rushed home and called you guys. I guess I should have notified you right from the start."

"Yes, I guess you should have."

Detective Gordon reached into his pocket for his cell phone. He called the precinct and reported the missing child. "Get a team over here right away—and bring the dog. I want him to sniff out the area before it starts raining so move it!"

While they waited for the officers to arrive, James Ballard continued with the rest of the story.

His wife threw a lavish party for the girls that afternoon to celebrate their thirteenth birthday. He wasn't able to attend: a board meeting at the bank ran longer than he expected. When he got home about six-fifteen, the party was over, the guests were gone, and his wife was just finishing cleaning up.

"I hadn't noticed Cindy's absence until Samantha called it to my attention," Ballard said, glancing at his daughter. "We were in the library. I'd been home about twenty minutes when Sam jumped up from her chair and ran to the window. She had been reading a new book someone had given her. She said something..." Again, Ballard's voice broke as he began to lose composure. He swallowed hard, and then started over. "She said something was wrong with Cindy. She wanted us to go look for her."

Gordon interrupted. "Why would she know Cindy was in trouble?"

Ballard stood and began to pace the floor. "They get these feelings about each other. Identical twins do that, you know."

The detective was skeptical, but he shrugged off Ballard's response with a positive tone. "Yeah, I've heard that about twins. So did you go out and look for her?"

"Right away. Sam stayed here with her mother—in case Cindy came home. I searched for over an hour, drove to the school and to a couple of her friends. Got back a little after eight. Bubbles..." Ballard paused, swallowed again and continued. "Bubbles had come home without her while I was gone."

"Bubbles?"

"The girls' dog."

Gordon hadn't noticed the shaggy little white mutt curled up under a chair in the corner. When Ballard mentioned her name, she crawled out and ran over to him.

"Mrs. Ballard, do you remember the time the dog came home?" Gordon asked.

The woman shook her head without looking up and began to weep. Ballard reached into his pocket, pulled out a handkerchief and handed it to her.

While waiting for the officers to arrive, Gordon continued to question Ballard and his wife. Having dismissed the possibility of foul play on the part of either of them, he was convinced this was a clear-cut kidnap case. Possibilities of who the abductor might be swam through his head. *Someone knew Ballard was well fixed and had singled him out as an easy take. An employee at his bank, maybe. Or a former employee: someone he had fired and was out for revenge.* All were possibilities that could be considered later. For now he needed to find a frightened thirteen-year-old that had just been kidnapped. He hoped it wouldn't prove to be a homicide case as well.

He had just started to talk to the twin when he heard the police cars pull up. She was still clinging to her knees, confused by what had happened and by all the commotion at such a late hour. "I'd like you to go for a ride with me, Samantha. Would you do that? Your mama can go, too. I'd like you to show me where you think your sister went."

She remained silent until her mother smiled and nodded her approval, then she lowered her feet to the floor. Clinging to her mother's hand, she slid off the sofa.

"Good girl," said the detective. "I'll talk to the police officers while you get your coats, then we'll go in my car."

The detective briefed the officers and instructed two of them to take Ballard and check out the school and the place where he had dropped the money. He asked the mother for a favorite stuffed animal of the missing child and was given a small teddy bear. *She slept with it every night for years,* he was told. Then they went to Gordon's car. Officer Ratcliff drove while the girl sat between him and the detective. Mrs. Ballard sat in the backseat. The other officer and the dog followed behind.

"You can call me Wes, Samantha," said the detective. "It's my job to find your sister, so I'm going to need all the assistance I can get. Will you help me?"

She nodded and asked, "Is the dog going to help, too?"

"He'll try. He might be able to smell where she has been, but we need you to show him where he should start looking."

As the two cars crawled through the neighborhood streets, Samantha instructed the officer when and where to turn. Gordon was beginning to feel they were wasting valuable time when suddenly the girl cried out. "Go there!" she said, as they approached a wooded area. "I think she rode her bicycle in there."

"Pull up," ordered Gordon. The four climbed out of the car. The officer with the dog pulled up behind them. "Turn him loose, Joe. She thinks she might have come in here."

Joe gave the dog one last sniff of the teddy bear and the dog charged off. It took no more than three minutes before his frantic barking beckoned for their attention; he had found Cindy's bicycle. The perp had shoved it between two tall bushes and taken the twin with him.

After calling the precinct for more help and cordoning off the area with crime scene tape, the officers began a thorough search for additional evidence.

Gordon was about to take Mrs. Ballard and her daughter back to the house when his cell phone rang. It was one of the officers who had taken James Ballard to the school and McKinley's Market. "Are you sitting down?" the officer said. "Because this one will blow you away. We've got the money. It was never picked up."

Two

He'd sat at the old picnic table too long recalling the past. The sun shifted its position and bathed him in glaring light. Rumpled and sweating, he stood up and removed his coat before heading back to his car. He slung the coat into the backseat as he climbed behind the steering wheel. In less than two hours he was to pick up Samantha.

Driving to his apartment, he remembered how determined he was to prove to O'Malley he was worthy of the case—even though he still felt inexperienced at the time. But most of all, he wanted to keep a promise he made to a little girl that he would find her sister. He felt he could keep that promise. Perhaps it had something to do with his own past that made him want the case, and he was determined to solve it. He had worked through the night searching for evidence, hoping to stumble onto something worthwhile. Finally, near morning, he was so exhausted he couldn't think. Reluctantly, he had gone home and fallen into bed just to be awakened by Chief O'Malley half-an-hour later.

☙ ❧

The ringing wouldn't stop. Without opening his eyes, he reached from under the blanket to silence it and knocked the phone to the floor. A muffled voice came from the receiver.

"Gordon? ... Gordon, answer the phone! Come on, I know you're there!"

The detective stretched out a naked arm and retrieved the instrument. "Yeah," he mumbled, still without opening his eyes.

It was O'Malley. The chief blared into his ear something about a car on fire up in the hills. "...no bodies, no one around."

"That's good," drawled the detective. He hung up the phone and put the pillow over his head.

The phone rang again, and again the naked arm reached out for it.

"Gordon! Wake up! It's connected!"

"I'm off Arson, O'Malley. Remember? You transferred me to homicide."

"It wasn't arson. Gordon, wake up! They found a kid's shoe—the size the Ballard kid would wear."

The detective's eyes flew open. In an instant, he was sitting on the edge of the bed, tangled in sheets and blankets. "What's that?"

"Better get down here: it might tie in with the kidnapping." The chief hung up.

Gordon charged up the rear steps of the precinct and through the back door. O'Malley was waiting for him in his office.

"Record time. I bet on twenty; you made it in sixteen."

"Cut the bull, O'Malley. What you got?"

Chief O'Malley shoved a chair in Gordon's direction with his foot. "Sit down. You'll like this."

The detective slouched into the chair, still exhausted from the previous twenty-four hours and no sleep. "Go on."

"Remember that call we got last night? From some woman up in the west hills: an explosion."

"No, O'Malley, I don't remember. I was on something more important." Gordon leaned his head back and closed his eyes.

"It was a car that had gone into the ravine—off Alderbrook Drive. Caught fire."

"Okay, so a car burned. Anybody hurt?"

"Nope. And nobody around when we got there. Nobody."

"What about the shoe? You said they found a shoe."

"We went back this morning to investigate, but the rain washed away evidence. Everything in the car burned,…" O'Malley pulled a shoe from his desk drawer and handed it over. "…but they found this shoe fifty feet from the scene."

Gordon's eyes opened. He sat up and took the shoe. It was new, but dirty and scratched. He rubbed off a crust of mud. Do we have a make on the car?"

"Not yet. They're towing it to Impoundment now. They'll call as soon as they've got something."

"When did it happen? What time?"

"About 10:20 PM."

"Fifteen minutes after the kidnapper called Ballard to drop the money." Gordon stood up. "I wanna go out there. Who's available?"

"Glad you asked. Your new partner's here. Gordon, see if you two can get along, okay?" The chief picked up the phone and pressed a button. "Carol, send Aguila in."

Gordon questioned his new partner during the short drive to the scene of the accident. His name was Juan Aguila and Gordon liked the guy. He was better looking and half-a-foot taller than himself, but he knew his place and was eager to learn. He was born and raised in Mexico and was a self-made man. Gordon had a hunch he would do his job well.

"You been up there?" asked the senior partner.

"Yeah, at sun-up."

"Find anything?"

"Only the shoe. The car was burned to a crisp. Some of the trees got singed, but it was still too wet to start a fire—lucky for the homes."

"Who found the shoe?"

"One of the officers."

"Know where?"

"Yeah, I'll show you when we get there. Turn here."

Gordon turned onto a narrow road.

"He went into the ravine."

"He?"

"Just guessing."

"Could have been a woman. Never assume till you know."

"Right. There was a dead deer."

"There's your reason."

"Yep. Pull over. It's down there," Aguila said, pointing.

The two men climbed from the car and started the descent down the embankment.

Aguila stopped. "Right here. This is where he found the shoe."

"Cursed rain. Washes away evidence." Gordon searched the area in spite of his pessimism. He found nothing. A wide strip of broken bushes and smashed weeds reflected where the charred car had been hauled back up onto the road. "Wish they hadn't got in a hurry. They're always in a hurry."

"There weren't no bodies. Didn't think it was foul play—with the deer and all. The driver probably jumped before it started down the embankment. Door was open."

"Then why hasn't he called in? He would have called in about his car." Gordon was disturbed. He was tired and needed more sleep. And the shoe bothered him.

After another fruitless search, the two men made their way back to the car. Gordon pulled out a map and marked their location with an X. "Let's talk to some neighbors? Know who called it in?"

"Yeah, somebody up in the hills there—just above us. I've got the address."

ଓ ༖

Gordon shook the memories from his head as he pulled up in front of his apartment, turned the wheels to the curb and set the brake. He looked at his watch: he had an hour before picking up Sam. He punched in the code to open the front door of the building and sprinted up the two flights of stairs.

With his hand on his gun, Gordon entered his apartment cautiously. It was a habit he had established after coming home late one night some months prior and finding it had been burglarized. It wasn't fancy, but it was roomy and it had a nice view. And it was *home*. It had been *home* to him for twelve years now, ever since he'd made detective.

He went straight to the bedroom, removed his clothes and threw them on the bed. In the bathroom, he turned the jet spray to its highest setting and stepped into the pounding water. He stood there trying to forget—but remembering—and cursing that day eleven years ago. He lifted his face to the cool spray, hoping the water would wash away the memories, the failures, the disappointments. It didn't. He turned the tap and the warmth took him back again to the day after the kidnapping.

03   80

"Okay, Gordon, what have you got? The FBI will be swarming all over the place soon, and I don't want them to think we're sitting on our hands."

The two detectives had been called into the chief's office immediately after he and Aguila had returned from the ravine. They told O'Malley they had searched the hillside where the car had burned looking for signs of life—a body could have been thrown a good distance at the time of the explosion—but there was no one. And, except for the black shoe, they found no other evidence.

They had questioned the woman who had called in. She and her husband were watching television when they heard the noise. From the window, they saw the fire down in the ravine. Neither she nor any of the neighbors had anything more to add.

"The shoe. What do you have on it?" O'Malley asked.

"Mostly mud," Gordon quipped with a wry smile. More seriously, he continued. "We went to the Ballard home and showed it to Mrs. Ballard. She was too upset to identify it, but the twin did. It was identical to a pair she had and she said they were both wearing them yesterday for the party. She said they often wore the same clothes."

"Okay, so now we've got something concrete. We know the kid was in the area," O'Malley concluded.

"What about the car?" Gordon asked.

"It was a Hertz rental. Check it out."

The girl at the Hertz desk showed them the rental slip. It was signed by a *Bill Jones* and was dated the morning of the kidnapping.

Gordon handed the slip back. "Did you ask for identification?"

The girl assured them that they had identified the man properly.

"What did the guy look like?"

She didn't know. She wasn't there then and the man that handled the transaction was in the hospital—sick.

"Then how do you know he was identified properly?" Aguila asked.

"Policy. We have a very strict policy: if we don't follow it, we get fired."

The two men got the name of the hospital and visited the sick Hertz agent, but he was unable to tell them anything about Bill Jones. The nurse said they were still running tests, but whatever he had affected his memory.

ଔ ଓ

Gordon looked at his watch, stepped out of the shower and dried himself. He dressed, straightened the bed and reached for a fresh coat. He looked at his watch again. Sam would be expecting him soon and he still hadn't decided what he would tell her.

He didn't want to think about it any longer. He had felt unequipped back then—far too inexperienced to work on a kidnapping, but O'Malley had confidence in him and kept him and Aguila on the case. But what more could someone else have done? They had searched the park thoroughly the night of the kidnapping—and again the next day. They had questioned the Ballard family, the neighbors, friends, and even Ballard's employees at the bank. They had followed up on every angle they could think of. Aguila had been a good partner and had even come up with ideas of his own, but they found nothing to lead them to Cindy Ballard.

And then the FBI arrived and told them to *butt out*. But they didn't. He and Aguila had continued to work on the case on their own. When they had time.

And as the months passed—and then the years— Gordon became discouraged and gave up. He had failed. The promise he made to Samantha would never be kept.

The day she went away to college, she never even called to say goodbye. That's when he made the decision to leave the case of Cynthia Ballard in the hands of the FBI where it belonged. He would forget Samantha Ballard existed. He would have to get on with his life.

Three

It took Gordon over an hour to drive from his apartment to the television studio in Lake Oswego. There was an accident on the freeway and by the time he pulled up to the curb, he was half an hour late. Samantha was standing there waiting. She wore a simple champagne-colored, two-piece dress that matched her hair perfectly, and she reminded him of Grace Kelly.

She had changed in the five years she had been away, but he would have known her had it been twenty. He still saw her face in his dreams too often. Perhaps it was guilt that kept the memory of her coming back—and the promise he never kept. He reached across and opened the door for her.

"I thought you would never come," she said as she slid across the seat and kissed him on the cheek. It was as if she had never been away. "You look marvelous, Wes. Your job must agree with you."

"It's okay. How does *Charley's* sound? They've remodeled, but the food is still good."

"*Charley's* is great! I'm starved." Sam twisted in the seat to get a better look at him. "I have *so much* to tell you, Wes. The past three years have been like a cyclone, what with college, the radio station, and now my new job with KSG-TV. It's all fitting in with my plans."

"What plans are those?"

She paused a moment, hesitating to answer. "Let's talk about you first. How's your job?"

"Same old routine: burglaries, shoplifting, stolen cars. Right now I'm on a case of a missing dog."

"You're kidding! A dog?"

"Yeah, some rich widow's prize poodle was stolen. She's offered five-thousand for it's return. It had four blue ribbons."

Sam laughed. It released the tension and he chuckled along with her.

He deliberately took the long route to Charley's. He had not yet recovered from the unexpected phone call that Sam was back and he didn't want to talk about Cindy. She was dead. He was sure of it, but he knew he would never convince Samantha of that.

By the time they reached the restaurant, the sun had set and a hundred moons reflected from the windows of the tall buildings. Ordinarily, Wes avoided the city whenever possible, but the food at Charley's was worth the fight through the freeway traffic—and the long drive delayed the inevitable.

He had made reservations for his favorite table next to a window overlooking the Willamette. The tablecloth was no longer the familiar red and white checks: it was soft blue and matched her eyes.

As he watched Sam ease into the chair held by the waiter, he was again reminded of Grace Kelly and how he had fallen in love with her after seeing *Dial M For Murder*. It occurred to him that it might have been the movie that made him want to become a police detective. He wondered if he had unknowingly transferred his youthful infatuation for the famous actress to Samantha.

They scanned the menus and Sam said, "Order for me, Wes. You know what I like."

"I know what you *used* to like. Has your taste changed?"

"I've learned to like escargot, but not tonight. Make it simple."

He could feel her eyes on him as he studied the menu. He ordered shrimp cocktail, a spinach salad and veal paprikash. He remembered her favorite food was veal.

"Perfect!" she said. "Not simple, but perfect."

Their salad plates were removed and replaced with the entrée before their conversation shifted from trivia to serious. They talked about Sam's new job and her desire to someday be an anchorwoman. For now, she would have to be content with writing copy and observing.

But not for long. Knowing you, Sam, you'll be right up there with the pros soon.

When Sam brought up the subject of Cindy, Wes remained silent for a while. He thought he had convinced himself not to get involved again, not to become a part of Sam's life, but when the words came out, they were not the ones he had rehearsed.

"Tell me about your plans, Sam."

She swallowed hard and laid her fork on the plate. "Television, Wes. It will take a while, but once my face is on the tube, maybe Cindy will see me and try to contact me."

So that's why she chose a TV career. Wes knew the time had come when he had to say what should have been said years ago. It would hurt, but it had to be done, and now was as good a time as any. He pushed his plate aside and reached across for her hand. Touching would make it easier. "Sam..." He paused and looked down, then tried again. "Sam, have you ever considered the possibility of..."

"Don't, Wes. I know what you're going to say. Cindy's alive. I *know* it. You can't give up. You promised."

"But, Sam, we haven't come up with anything in years. Neither we nor the FBI have developed any new positive leads. There just *isn't* anymore evidence!"

"There is!" Sam shouted. Wes was upset again. He would be even more upset when he heard about the letter she had slipped into her handbag before leaving for work that morning, the letter she had received just before leaving for college. She had never shown it to anyone, but she had decided it was time to give it to Wes. She reached down for the bag that was sitting by her feet and placed it in her lap, then put it back on the floor. *I can't,* she thought. *I can't risk it. Not yet.*

"What do you mean—there is? You've found something?"

Sam dropped her eyes. She had to say something—something to convince him the case should be reopened. She put her fist to her chest and said, "It's in here, Wes. I can still *feel* her. If she were dead, I wouldn't be able to *feel* her. You can't believe that, can you?"

Angry and disappointed he pushed back in his chair. "I've tried. Believe me, I've tried, but it just didn't get me anywhere. I tried for six years, Sam."

"Is that why you gave up? Because you couldn't *feel* her as I do?" Sarcastically, she added, "Or was it because I left?"

"No, that's not it! I..." People began to stare. Wes lowered his voice. "I ran out of clues, that's all. And you never even said goodbye."

"I wanted to, believe me, I did. But you were acting like you didn't want to have anything more to do with me."

"It wasn't that. It was...I was sure that..."

"That she was dead, I know. You gave up." Samantha stood. "Then I'll have to do it alone, but, I'm going to find her, Wesley Gordon! She's out there somewhere. Why she doesn't try to contact us, I don't know, but there's a reason and I want to know what it is!" She started to stalk away.

"Wait!" He pulled a couple of bills from his wallet and threw them on the table, then followed her out of the restaurant. Outside, he grabbed her by the arm. "Sam, wait! Let me explain!"

She stopped, then turned and looked at him for a moment. There were tears in her eyes. He put his arms around her to comfort her, just as he had done so many times when she was a little girl. Words were left unsaid.

She looked up. "I've missed you, Wes. You never answered my letters: you stopped writing."

"Yeah, well, I...stopped a lot of things. Let's go to the car, and you can tell me about your plans."

Four

They drove into the hills not far from her childhood home and parked. The glimmer of the city lights reflecting on the night clouds gave the appearance of daylight. He shut off the engine and turned to look at his passenger. Her face glowed in the illumination and she looked like the porcelain doll again. *Just a child*, he thought, *frightened and insecure. Would she ever grow up? Would she ever be a woman?* Wes shook the thoughts from his head. What did it matter to him....now?

The silence was broken by a carload of teenagers passing by with their boom box at ear-shattering decibels. Samantha put her hands over her ears until the noise was gone.

"There was a time when I enjoyed that," she said, frowning. "Remember the night I talked you into taking me to the *Pagan Paupers* concert? I was...how old? Sixteen?"

"Fifteen. It was your birthday and you bugged out on your friends."

"I remember. Nine years ago. You hated every minute, but you never said a word." Solemnly, she said, "What happened, Wes?"

"What do you mean?"

"You've changed. Back then you were a ball of fire, filled with spunk and zest for life. Nothing could stop you. You were going to be the best detective on the force, remember?"

"I got old, I guess."

"No, you didn't get old, you *made* yourself old." Samantha reached for his hand. "Wes, you're only thirty-seven. You have a whole life ahead of you, but you put it in a basket and threw it away."

She didn't sound like a child anymore. Maybe she has grown up. "Tell me more about your plans," he said, changing the subject.

"I want to talk about you first. What's happened to you? You used to love police work."

"It's okay, but I'm tired, I guess. Tired of being shot at, tired of the pace, tired of kids high on drugs, tired of...I don't know."

Disappointed, Samantha let go of his hand and looked down.

"Don't do that to me, Sam." It was the woe-be-gone look he had seen so many times when she was a child that got to him.

She looked up and into his eyes without speaking, once again a child.

"All right, you win! I'll see what I can do, but there's got to be something new to reopen the case—something more than just your premonitions."

Wes had never been fully convinced the feelings Sam got when she was a child—and later—could be helpful in finding her sister. He was a skeptic, but he knew it gave her hope, and hope was what she needed to get her through school and on through life, so he humored her. He had never allowed himself to become attached to people—until he met Sam. She wasn't like other kids—so many of them spoiled and bratty. She was different.

"...but it was the dream...Wes, are you listening?"

"Sorry, Kitten..." There, he had slipped. He was determined he was not going to call her the pet name he had given her when she was a child. It made things too personal again. "...I drifted, Sam. What were you saying?"

"You're not really interested, are you?"

"I am. Go on. Tell me about your premonition."

"Like I was saying...It wasn't really a premonition this time, it was a dream—about a month ago. But when I woke up, I had this very strong feeling it was real and I couldn't shake it. Wes, I dreamed about Maria."

"Maria? Who's Maria?"

"You know, the woman who took care of us when we were kids—when we were little and Mom worked."

Wes perked up. "You never told me about her."

"We did. Surely, we did. Don't you remember? It was the day after Cindy was kidnapped, and you were asking about all the people that worked with Dad at the bank and about Mom's friends and..." Her voice trailed; she was straining to remember. "Wes, maybe they didn't."

"They didn't, Sam. I wouldn't forget. I must have gone over the file a thousand times. Tell me about her."

Samantha frowned and started to bite her nails, then stopped as Wes reached out to pull her hand away. She searched her memory for the time when Maria started working for her parents. "It was...I think we were four. Mom took a job and they hired Maria to take care of us. She lived across town. I remember, because she took us to her home one day, and that made Dad very angry. He fired her."

"How old were you then?"

"Eight. No, nine. Then a couple of years later, when we were in the sixth grade, they moved into our neighborhood."

"They?"

"She had married and they bought a condo a few blocks from us. She came to visit us one day, but Dad wouldn't let her in."

Wes remained silent for a moment, thinking. "You'd have been eleven—two years before Cindy was kidnapped." He continued to contemplate, and then suddenly asked, "Sam, how did this woman treat you? Did you like her?"

"Cindy liked her more than I did, but she was partial to Cindy. It is one of the few times we differed in opinion. Wes, surely you don't think..."

"What did her husband do? For a living?"

"He was a salesman of some kind. He came to our house once to try to sell us something—insurance, I think. I remember he was well-dressed and quite handsome."

Wes shifted his position. "Do you have any pictures of Maria?"

"Mom probably does. She was always taking pictures."

"I want you to find one for me. And I want Maria's and her husband's full names and their address."

"They don't live there anymore. They moved long ago."

"Then get me the address of the condo. First thing tomorrow?"

It had been a long time since Wesley Gordon had felt fire in his veins, but now, with this new information about the twins' babysitter, he felt he had something to work with. Silently, he cursed himself for not knowing about her before. He had followed every lead possible, back then, eleven years ago. He had looked into the lives of every person connected to the family that could have held a grudge and it netted him nothing. But he was never told about Maria. He wondered why.

Five

Gordon parked in the south lot across from the precinct, bounced from his car and crossed the street. He entered the building and caught an elevator just as the door was closing. Records were kept on the eleventh floor. He pressed the button.

It was still early. O'Malley would not be in for at least an hour. He wanted to review the case before the chief arrived, to be prepared for the argument he knew he would get from him. Opening the case of Cynthia Ballard at a local level would not sit well with him. *It's in the hands of the FBI,* he would say. *They never close a case until it's solved.* But Gordon knew they had ceased to work on it long ago.

He asked the clerk for the Cynthia Ballard file and headed back to his office hoping to be unseen.

He'd been privileged to have his own office for nearly a year now, and although small, it was away from the constant comings and goings of the other detectives. There were no windows—Gordon loved to look out over the city when he was pensive—but he had hung a painting on the wall opposite his desk that was a fair substitute.

He switched on the desk light and settled into the pillow-stuffed chair he had brought from home to replace the hardback desk chair typical of a police station. Comfortable, he opened the file and started to read. He read and then read it over and over again for nearly an hour.

Gordon turned out the desk light, leaned back and closed his eyes. For the first time in five years, he mulled over the facts.

He and Aguila had stayed on the case long after the FBI had given up and gone home. They had questioned nearly a hundred people, and then questioned them again. Except Maria. Why had no one ever mentioned the twins' baby-sitter? Could that information have been left out of the file? No, he was sure she had never been mentioned.

Weary, his thoughts returned to the day Samantha graduated from high school.

ଔ ଝ

"And now we will hear from the class valedictorian, our very own Samantha Ballard!"

While the audience cheered, Samantha arose from her chair and with an air of dignity and self-confidence walked to the microphone. Her sky-blue eyes were misty with emotion. Her long golden curls had been cut to shoulder length and, though still petite, she was now a beautiful young lady. The applause continued until she raised her hands to signal *enough.*

"Mr. Chambers, members of the faculty, fellow-students, family and friends, today is the day we, the Class of '93, have so anxiously awaited. We have set goals..."

Later, at the open house, Gordon walked up to Samantha and put his arm around her shoulders. "Your speech was terrific, Sam! You made me and your Dad very proud of you."

Samantha smiled with satisfaction and kissed him on the cheek. She had come to think of him as the big brother she always wanted but never had. They talked a while until her father approached.

"Hey there, young lady, your guests are wondering when they are going to get to talk to you. You'd better mingle." Sam's father bubbled with pride as he ushered his daughter away from Gordon and toward a group of her peers. She was soon enveloped by her friends and was deep into conversation and laughter.

Ballard walked back to Gordon, still standing alone by the table with a punch cup in his hand.

Gordon set the cup on the table. "She's a lovely girl, Jim. I wonder where she'll go from here?"

"She could go a long way, if she could forget about her mother and Cindy. It's the only way she'll ever make it."

"She'll still go far, even then."

Ballard filled a punch cup and took a sip. "You're in love with her, aren't you, Wes?"

Gordon was shocked at Ballard's accusation. "Jim, she's just a kid."

"Not anymore. Does she know? Have you told her?"

"No, of course not! Well, she knows I'm very fond of her but..."

"Take it easy, Wes. I just wanted you to know how I feel about it. You're right: she's too young to get romantically involved. I'm glad you realize that." Jim walked away and left him standing alone—wondering.

଼ ଽ

Gordon shook his head and had just opened his eyes when the ceiling light went on. Chief O'Malley stood in the doorway.

"You here? Don't you like lights?"

"I wanted to go over a file before you arrived. Sit down, Chief. I've got something new."

"On what? What case—the dog?" asked the chief as he pulled up the hardback chair the detective had abandoned.

"The Ballard kidnapping."

"No, not again, Gordon. I thought you had gotten over that obsession."

"I did, but Sam's back."

"What's that got to do with it?"

"Last night she told me something we never knew before—something important. I want to reopen the case, Chief."

"You're joking. What could be so important after all these years? The kid's dead: you know the statistics." He leaned back in the chair, braced his head in his hands and propped his feet on the desk.

"Maybe she is, maybe she isn't. There was a baby-sitter: she took care of the twins for four, maybe five years. Then Ballard fired her." Gordon waved the file at his chief. "But, no one ever mentioned her, Chief." The detective slammed the file back down on the desk and stood up.

The chief looked mildly interested. "When was she fired? How old were the kids then?"

Gordon was pacing. "Sam says they were eight or nine. She doesn't remember."

The chief shot forward. "Four years before the abduction! They had probably forgotten about her."

Wes sat down again and looked the chief in the eye. "No, they kept showing up…"

"They?"

"Yeah, she got married and they moved into the Ballard neighborhood just a year or so before Cindy was taken. I want to check it out, Chief. I want to know why no one ever mentioned the babysitter."

Six

The drive from her apartment in Lake Oswego to her childhood home in the West hills of Portland seemed longer than it did five years ago. *Traffic's thicker now,* she thought. Her father had invited her to live with him, but she had been away too long and was too independent to accept his hospitality. *It wouldn't be the same, without Cindy and Mom*, she reasoned.

As Samantha eased past merging traffic, she thought about the letter in her handbag. She had intended to give it to Wes the night before, but changed her mind when she recalled the threat the writer had made. *Your sister is gone! Accept it, or you will end up like your mother, and Gordon will be dead!* The letter continued with further warnings if she ever revealed its presence to anyone.

It had been mailed from Beaverton—dropped in a roadside box, no doubt. It looked like it had been typed on a cheap, old-fashioned typewriter that hadn't been cleaned in years. The closed letters were filled solid with ink from the ribbon and they were not evenly spaced. Even the wording was childish.

Sam dismissed it as being sent by a prankster. Nevertheless, rather than destroy it, she kept it hidden away in a small box in her closet. It never occurred to her at the time that it might lead to her sister.

Samantha pulled into the driveway just as her father returned from his morning jog. He reached her car door before she had a chance to open it herself.

"Morning, love. You got here early." He planted a kiss on her cheek and helped her out of the car.

"I left my apartment at eight. It seemed to take hours. I wanted to catch you before you went to work."

"Not going to work. I have a plane to catch. Banker's convention in Reno."

Samantha flinched as they entered the house and the memory of her sister came back to her. She followed her father up the winding staircase, recalling the many times they were scolded for sliding down the banister.

"Dad, do you know where Mom kept the photos of us when we were little?"

"No, love, I don't, but you can look in the closet under the stairs. I'd bet on that."

"And if they're not there?"

Ballard paused before entering the master suite. "Your guess is as good as mine. I haven't moved anything since the day your mother left."

"You should, you know. It's time you got rid of some of the junk." Sam ran her finger across the hall commode and checked it for dust. "And you really do need a housekeeper, Dad. Will you let me find one for you?"

"I do just fine. She'll come back someday and she wouldn't want a stranger changing things."

Samantha followed her father into the bedroom. "I love you, Dad, and I don't want to hurt you, but it's time you realized: she's not coming back."

"You don't know."

"Dad, it's been eleven years."

"Only ten. She's...undergoing treatment."

Sam knew how painful it was for him to discuss his wife, her mother. The shock of Cindy's disappearance had been more than she could handle: she crawled into a shell and never came out. It had been difficult for her father to lose a daughter, then a wife.

More so than it had been for Sam. She *knew* her sister would come back someday, in spite of what the letter had said. She didn't have that much hope for her mother's return.

"I'm going to shower, then I'm off." Ballard pulled his sweatshirt over his head and threw it on a chair. "Why don't you stay here while I'm gone?"

"Maybe I will. I have the weekend off." *And it will give me a chance to clean house*, she thought as she watched the sweatshirt fall to the floor.

"Have you had breakfast?" Ballard yelled from the bathroom.

"No, I'll grab something later. Wes and I had a wonderful meal at Charley's last night and I'm still stuffed."

"How is Wes?" Ballard yelled again as he turned on the shower.

"Doing fine, Dad. He's going to..." She decided not to tell her father Wes had agreed to reopen Cindy's case. It would just upset him.

Sam went to the closet her father had mentioned and opened the door. Inside were a number of boxes, all neatly stacked and labeled. She started pulling them out. By the time her father had dressed and was ready to leave, she had gone through every box there. There were no photographs.

"I struck zero, Dad," she said as he kissed her goodbye. "Any ideas?"

"Try the garage. Gotta go, love."

She decided to fix herself a cup of coffee before searching further. As she sat at the kitchen table sipping the hot liquid, she imagined herself once again as a child. For a brief moment she saw Cindy standing on a chair next to her mother mixing batter for a cake, and she felt a pang of jealousy. Cindy had loved to cook, just like their mother. It had not been Sam's favorite pastime so she had often been left out. *My own fault*, she thought. *I should have shown more interest.*

She put the cup in the sink and headed for the garage.

She had gone through several boxes before she found one labeled *scrapbooks*. She pulled it from its place and lifted it onto a workbench. The first two books held snapshots of her parents, their friends, relatives and some people she didn't know.

The third book was filled with photos of herself and Cindy. She smiled as she touched the one of her father holding a twin in each arm. His grin stretched from ear to ear, and Sam laughed aloud as she brushed a tear from her cheek.

She studied each picture as she turned the pages—remembering, longing for the companionship of *her other half*, as she often called her. Moments of fun and laughter they had so often experienced filled her thoughts. Briefly, unpleasant events returned, but she pushed them from her mind.

It was the photo of herself and Cindy—they were hugging each other—that brought on the feeling. It was stronger than ever before. She could *feel* Cindy's presence. She looked up quickly expecting to see her standing there. But, she was not there. And yet she was. Her head began to pound as she heard Cindy's voice call out to her. *Sam, I'm here. I'm here.* She reached out to touch her, but there was no one there.

Samantha looked out the garage window at the swing set where she and Cindy had spent so much time pushing each other. It had become rusty with age, and one swing was missing the seat. She looked again at the scrapbook and touched the photo, but the feeling was gone.

She remembered her mission: to find a photo of Maria. *There has to be at least one. Mother was always taking pictures of us,* she thought. Then she saw the place where one had been removed. She continued searching and noticed three more missing photos, but found none of Maria.

She flinched as she came to one of Cindy and her holding Mickey Mouse's hand. For their eighth birthday, their parents had taken them to Disneyland. It was fun at the park, but the memory of that night in the hotel came back to her—and the fight her parents had after they had gone to bed. It was not a happy thought.

ଔ ଞ

"I want you to get rid of her!" he yelled. "I don't trust her."

"But, Jim, she's so good with the children."

"We'll find someone else. No, you can stay home and take care of them yourself. You don't need to work: you never did."

"But I enjoy my job—it's only part-time—and the girls are well cared for."

"You'll do as I say!"

"All right, Jim! But lower your voice. The girls will hear you."

ଔ ଞ

Sam shook the scene from her head and closed the book. She returned it to the box and took it back to its place in the corner of the garage. Time was passing quickly. Wes would be expecting her at La Casita for lunch, and she still had to drive by the condo and get the address. She was not sure how she would find Maria's married name—or that of her husband—but she remembered the condo. It was blue, next to a yellow one on the right. It would be easy to locate.

She returned to the house for her handbag, but it was not in sight. *Where did I leave it?* she thought as she scolded herself for being so careless. She found it on the upstairs hall commode, grabbed it and left the house.

It took only a few moments to drive to the area where Maria had lived with her new husband, but she was not prepared for what she saw. The condominiums had been painted gray with white trim. They all looked alike.

Seven

He had arrived early knowing there would be a line, and had just been seated when she came through the door. He waved.

Sliding into the booth, she asked, "Did you talk to Chief O'Malley? Did he consent to let you reopen Cindy's case?"

Pushing the menu aside, he leaned across the table. "He agreed, but only if I can show him some new evidence. Did you bring a photo of Maria?"

"I couldn't find one, Wes: I looked for hours. There weren't any of her."

"But you said..."

"I know, and it's true. Mom was always carrying the camera around. But there were none of Maria."

"How about the address? And their names?"

"I drove to the area, but the condos all look alike now. I couldn't decide which one was theirs. And I can't remember her married name. I struck out, Wes, didn't I?"

He leaned back and picked up the menu again. "I'm having enchiladas and a relleno. What do you want?"

Sam knew Wes was upset with her, but it wasn't her fault. She had tried to carry out her mission—to find a photo of Maria and get her name and address—but circumstances prevented it. Undecided and lacking an appetite, she reluctantly ordered a combination plate and soft drink.

Wes finished his lunch long before Sam ate half of hers. He hardly spoke throughout the entire meal. Pushing her food aside, she said, "I had another premonition, Wes. It was while I was going through the photos. She came to me and said, *Sam, I'm here. I'm here.* I could feel her with me again, Wes. Please don't be angry."

He wiped his mouth with his napkin and took a sip of coffee. "I'm not mad at you, Kitten. It's just that my hands are tied—without new evidence. O'Malley doesn't consider *premonitions* to be evidence."

"But you said Maria is new evidence."

"She's a suspect, Sam, only a suspect. And it's a long shot at that." The disappointment in her expression prompted him to continue. "Relax. We'll find her. If she worked for your parents for five years, she *did* exist—unless you dreamed her up."

Wes's last comment hit a nerve and Sam shot out of her seat. "What do you mean, *dreamed her up?* You don't believe me!"

He grabbed her by the hand and pulled her back into the booth. "I believe you; I was just horsing around. What time do you have to go to work?"

Without looking at him, she answered, "Four."

"Then we've got plenty of time. Let's go."

After climbing into Wes's car, Samantha asked, "Where are we going?"

"To the bank. I want to talk to your father."

"He's not there: he flew to Reno. Banker's convention."

Wes slammed his hand onto the steering wheel. He made a sudden U-turn in the middle of the street and headed the other direction. Sam's handbag flew to the floor and its contents were strewn about.

"Now, where we going?" she asked, gathering them together.

"To your house."

Sam hesitated to ask what they could possibly find at the Ballard home that would shed any light on the case. He had that determined look and she knew by experience it meant he would not answer. She decided to be patient.

They arrived within minutes and entered the home. Baffled by his intentions, Sam waited, his expression telling her he had a plan—that he knew exactly why he was there and what he was after. It soon became evident.

"Where do your folks keep their bank records: old ones?"

"I...I have no idea."

"Well, guess!" Wes was irritated again, but this time his acrid response boomeranged.

Disparagingly, she shot back, "How old, Your Honor?"

Wes paused to calculate, then answered more civilly. "1982. You would have been six years old. Right?"

She had made her point—and had brought him to his knees. "Yes, six. Maybe they're in the garage—that old. If they were kept this long."

"He's a banker. Bankers never throw out anything."

It took only ten minutes for them to find the stack of boxes that held old financial records. He was right: there were boxes that dated back to 1974, the year her parents were married.

He found one marked 1982 and pulled it out. It contained a journal, old receipts—each neatly marked *paid* and organized in folders—and bank statements. "Bingo!" he shouted. "Help me look through these. I want a check made out to Maria."

So that's what he's after, she thought. Hesitantly, she asked, "What if they paid cash?"

"Uh-uh, not a banker. He'd be doing things by the book. Start looking." He handed her an envelope filled with cancelled checks."

Within moments, they each found one made out to *Maria Gonzales* and signed by her father. Both checks had a note written in the lower left corner: one read *February babysitting*, the other, *March babysitting*. He turned them over and looked at the endorsement: they were deposited at First Bank of Oregon. Scribbling the account number on a pad, he noted the checks were not drawn from Ballard's own bank. Curious, he concluded that he did not want his employees to know his financial business. *Makes sense,* he thought. But he made a mental note.

Sam interrupted. "Wes, I've got to go. I'll be late for work."

Stuffing the checks back into the envelopes, he replacing them in the box, then lifted it back into its place on the shelf. "Okay, Kitten. I'll drop you off at your car. I've got what I came for."

Eight

The drive to the studio was steady but slow and she had to fight to stay awake. Suddenly the taillights ahead of her turned red. Throwing on her brakes, she came to a stop within inches of a pickup. "Not an accident. Please, God, don't let it be an accident," she said aloud, glancing upward.

She looked at her watch. The delay stretched from two minutes into ten. Leaning forward, she placed her head on her hands still locked around the steering wheel. Her eyes closed and she saw Maria.

CB ВО

"You girls be good now and mind your mother. Come here, Sam, and give me a kiss." Maria stooped and took the child into her arms. She held her briefly while she kissed both cheeks, then released her and turned to her sister. Cindy ran into her outstretched arms. "I'm going to miss you, Cindy; I'm going to miss you terribly. I'm even going to miss the tricks you girls play on me."

"You can't go, Maria. It's not fair. You didn't do nothing wrong." Cindy burst into tears.

Through her own tears, Maria corrected her. "*Anything*, Cindy. I didn't do *anything* wrong. You must learn to speak correctly if you want to be important someday."

CB ВО

"...*want to be important someday...important someday... important...*"

The blasting of the horns jolted her awake and she eased her foot onto the gas pedal. Glancing at her watch, she realized she had drifted into a dream state for twenty minutes. She would be late for work.

The day dragged. Sam liked her new job, but she hadn't been on camera yet and she was bored with just writing copy and observing. She felt she was ready for more responsibility; she wanted to be on camera.

After work, she planned on going straight to her former home—she still thought of it as *home*—but decided better of it and chose the short trip to her apartment. Entering, she paused to listen to the silence. A clock somewhere ticked away the after-midnight moments and she realized how much she missed her sister.

As she crawled into bed, she tried to visualize what her sister would look like now, then chided herself when she remembered that all she had to do was look into a mirror and she would see her. Perhaps with sufficient intent, she would be able to *feel* her again as she did earlier that morning and she immersed herself in deep concentration. Nothing came and she fell asleep.

The radio blasted to life at the precise hour of seven. She had forgotten to re-set it. She stretched forth her hand and, fumbling, turned it off. Six hours of restless sleep were not enough, she concluded as she pulled the blanket around her ears and sank back into the pillow.

She had just started dreaming when the telephone rang. Again, she reached out from under the blankets and touched the *off* button of the radio. The jingling continued until she realized it was the phone. She picked up the receiver and put it to her ear. "Hello," she squeaked.

"Sam, is that you?"

One eye flipped open. "Wes?"

"Yeah, did I wake you?"

"No, I'm still asleep." The eye closed again.

"Wake up, kid. I need your help."

"I just crawled into bed. Can't it wait?"

"It's ten-thirty. Get up; we've got work to do."

Sam flung the blanket back and sat up, legs dangling over the bedside. "What? Did you find something?"

"Enough to convince O'Malley to let me work on it. I'll pick you up in a half-hour. Be ready." The line went dead.

The hot shower brought her back to life and she began to feel the excitement that once again seemed to encompass Wes. She was eager to know what he had uncovered. Her skin tingled as it grew red from the steaming water. Realizing she had allowed it to become too hot, she switched to *cold* and jumped back at the sudden change. It was while she was drying herself with the towel that she remembered a moment in the past. They were seven.

ଓଃ ଚଠ

"Mommy, why is my mole on the left and Sam's on the right?"

Carla Ballard patted her daughter dry, then turned to her twin sister and began rubbing her with the towel. "Because you are *mirror* twins, my dear. But the mole is the only thing you have that's different—that we know of, that is."

"Is Sam's heart on the other side?"

Their mother laughed. "No, it's on the left where it belongs."

"But, why? It should be on the right."

"That's very good reasoning for a seven-year-old. We'll have to ask the doctor the next time we see him. Here, put these on, girls." Their mother handed them each a pair of identical pink panties trimmed with white lace.

Cindy slipped into hers with ease, then pulled them down again on the left side and looked with curiosity at the mole on her hip. "Someday I'll have mine taken off. It's ugly."

Her sister slapped her hand. "No! It has to stay there. I like mine and if you have yours taken off, I will have to do it, too."

"You don't!" shrieked Cindy. "We don't *always* have to do everything just alike, do we, Mommy?"

"Of course not, love. As you grow older, you'll be different. You'll dress differently, your hair can be different and you'll even want to do different things."

"No!" protested Sam. "We are the same! We will always be the same! I don't want to be different!"

ൟ ൠ

Sam finished drying herself, then looked down at the mole on her hip. She wondered if Cindy had ever had hers removed.

Nine

Wes's car was waiting in front when Sam glanced out the living room window. The sky had darkened and looked ominous. As she reached into the coat closet, she wondered if Wes had truly discovered something worthwhile, or if it would be another false lead like the many useless bits of information he had accumulated years ago. Preparing herself for disappointment, she opened the front door. Wes had his finger on the doorbell.

"Good. You're ready," he mumbled as he grabbed her by the elbow and led her down the stairs. "Good thing you wore a coat, radio says it's going to rain. 'Bout time."

He helped her into the car and as he walked around to the driver's side, she noticed the teddy bear stuffed between the seats. She pulled it out and fingered it.

Wes climbed in and started the car. "O'Malley called the FBI. They..." He sensed something wrong and before pulling away from the curb turned to find Sam holding the bear close to her breast. "What it is, Kitten?" Sam didn't answer. "What... what's wrong?"

She continued to ignore him. Her eyes were closed and her knuckles were white from gripping the bear so tightly. He waited. He wished he'd returned it to the drawer where it belonged; it brought back memories that were too painful for her.

In the distant sky, a streak of lightning warned of a pending storm. A clap of thunder followed, but Sam remained oblivious.

Wes grew nervous and touched her arm. "Sam." She didn't respond so he shook her gently. "Samantha." Still, there was no response.

A second report, this time louder, preceded the downpour. She dropped the bear into her lap and opened her eyes. For a moment, she appeared disoriented, confused. Wes cupped his hand under her chin and turned her head towards him. "Hey, Kitten, are you okay?" He had never seen her like this before.

She reached out, flung her arms around him and clung tightly. Wes was baffled: something was wrong, very wrong. This was more than nostalgia, more than just *memories of her sister*. Wes waited.

Tightening her grip, Samantha bellowed, "It's Cindy again: she's in trouble! She called out to me! Wes, we have *got* to find her soon!"

For the first time, he witnessed one of her premonitions. He always doubted them before, but this was real. He sensed it; he knew it. Something bound the two girls together just as she said. She was right all along. He felt ashamed that he always scoffed. Until now.

Still clinging to her, he whispered into her ear. "We'll find her, Sam, you and me. We'll find her."

Wes pulled into a drive-in and asked for two cups of coffee. The thunderstorm had subsided and now the rain tapped lightly on the windshield. He passed the coffee to her, pulled into a parking space and turned off the engine.

He waited for the hot liquid to take effect and then he turned to her. "Feeling better?"

"Uh-huh." Her response was barely audible.

"Want to talk about it?"

"Not now. Tell me what you found."

Wes set his cup on the dashboard and pulled some notes from his shirt pocket. "The checks we found: a judge declared them competent evidence. He gave me a writ and I got copies of Maria's bank statements. Look at this." He held a paper in front of her and pointed. "Look here. She signed as Maria Gonzales, but over here...a year later..." Wes shuffled the papers. "...she signed as Maria Corelli."

Sam interrupted. "That would be about when she got married, long after Dad fired her."

"But look at this. She made out her last check to open a new account at another bank and deposited a couple o' hundred dollars." Again Wes shuffled the papers. "Here's a page from the new bank statement. Your Maria got lucky, Miss Ballard. She didn't marry a salesman, she married a doctor."

Sam took the page from his waving hand. The account was in the names of Maria Corelli and Anthony Corelli, M.D. Furrowing her brow, she said, "Then this means Maria didn't kidnap Cindy—at least not for money. It's another dead end, Wes."

"Not necessarily. It's not true that all doctors are millionaires, you know." Holding up a paper, Wes returned to the subject of the bank account. "Look at this statement. In April, they only had a little over a thousand dollars in that account. That's not much money, but Corelli probably had another account somewhere. Now, look at this one: deposits are sporadic and in different amounts, but just a few months later, the account is up to over twenty-three thousand dollars. Four months in a row, there's a deposit of exactly twenty-five hundred around the fifteenth of every month. Sam, those deposits were made the four months just prior to Cindy's abduction. They stopped after she was kidnapped."

"What does that mean?"

"You tell me. Maybe they..."

Sam interrupted. "Wes, the burned car...Do you still think whoever kidnapped Cindy was on his way to pick up the money and drop Cindy off, but had an accident?"

"I'm sure of it." Wes brought up the shoe. "Otherwise, why would it have been there?"

"But what could have happened to her? And to the kidnapper?"

"I wish I knew."

She drained her cup and crumpled it in her hand. Wes's theories were not new. They had discussed them many times before when Sam was old enough to understand—and reason—but Maria had never entered their conversation. Now, with the twins' former babysitter as a suspect, everything took on a new perspective.

"Then *he* could have been a *her*. Maria could have been the kidnapper. But why, Wes? Why would she take Cindy?"

"For the money, I guess. But what makes you think it was *just* Maria? Maybe Corelli was there, too. Or...maybe Corelli did the dirty work. Maybe Maria had nothing to do with it."

Sam frowned again and shook her head. "No, Wes, I just can't believe Maria was involved. She loved my mother, they were very close." Sam shook her head with even more conviction. "She wouldn't have done that to her. And a doctor! What would they have to gain?" She tapped the bank statement with her finger. "If they had *that* much, he must have been successful. They probably had other accounts, as well. They wouldn't *need* ransom money."

"You could be right, but I'm not willing to write them off yet. I want to know why the twenty-five hundred dollar deposits—where did the money come from?"

He started the car and pulled onto the street. Sam was thrown to the right. "Where are we going?" she asked.

"To your house."

"Again? Dare I ask why?"

"I want to search the place while your Dad's gone. Do you mind?"

"Not if it will help find Cindy, but what are we looking for?"

"I'm not sure yet. Anything that might give us a lead. I've got to come up with more than we've got to convince the FBI to re-open the case."

"I thought you said they never close a case until it's solved."

"They don't, officially, but they're known to shelve it when the leads run out."

The traffic on Interstate Five was flowing smoothly and the twenty-five minutes it took to drive to the Ballard home went quickly. Neither spoke during the trip. Both were ensconced in their own private thoughts. Before Sam realized the time had passed, Wes was pulling onto the street where she had grown up.

"We're here already?" she said, looking up in astonishment.

"Doesn't take long when you're in good company."

"Are you referring to *you* or *me*?" Sam didn't wait for an answer. Glancing up the street toward her former home, she said, "Wes, someone is pulling away from our house. Can you catch up with them?"

"Probably a salesman: could be anyone." Pressing hard on the accelerator, they lunged forward. "Too late. They've turned the corner. Seem to be in an awful big hurry. I wouldn't worry about it, Sam."

Not sure about his last statement, Wes was tempted to follow the car, then thought better of it and pulled into the driveway. Mrs. Hatch, long-time neighbor of the Ballards, called out to them from across the street when they got out of the car.

"It's good to see you back, Samantha. Wes, is that you? It's been years."

The two walked across the street to greet her less formally. "It's nice to be home, Mrs. Hatch, but I'll only be staying a couple of days while Dad is away. I have an apartment in Lake Oswego near the studio. Did Dad tell you I have a job there?" Sam pulled her coat collar up as the rain drops began to slither down her neck.

"Yes, my dear. He told me all about it. You always did get what you wanted, didn't you?"

Wes was impatient. Idle chatter bored him and he interrupted before Sam had a chance to answer. "Mrs. Hatch, the car that just pulled away: did you notice who it was?"

"That's why I came out. I was at my kitchen window when I saw him leave your house."

"Leave our house!" shrieked Sam.

"Yes, he seemed to know what he was doing so I wasn't concerned—until he started to get into his..."

Again, Wes interrupted. "What made you suspicious?"

"His hat: he had it pulled down to cover his face. And he had on a raincoat. It was as if he didn't want to be recognized. But then it is raining, you know." Mrs. Hatch stepped back a few steps on her front porch to avoid getting wet.

"Are you sure he came out of the house?"

"Absolutely! And he looked around to see if anyone was watching."

"Did you get the license plate number?" Wes asked the question expecting the *no* that followed. "Come on, Sam, let's check the house." Turning back to thank the woman, he asked one last question. "Are you sure it was a man?"

Mrs. Hatch remained fixed. Thinking carefully, she responded, "No, I can't be sure. It could have been a woman."

Ten

They checked each room for disturbance, nothing was out of place or missing. Every room appeared untouched.

"Look again, Sam," Wes said. "Someone wanted something or they wouldn't have entered the house."

"Unless it was a friend of Dad's who came to see him."

"With a key? Maybe. Do you know where he's staying?"

"No, but his secretary would. Want me to call her?"

"Yeah, call her."

It took only two phone calls to get Mr. Ballard on the line. The hotel was also hosting the banker's convention so Sam asked the operator to page him.

"It's me, Dad. Wes and I are at the house. Hate to disturb you, but something has come up. Does anyone have a key to the house other than you and me?"

She shook her head slowly to convey the answer to Wes.

"Think carefully, Dad. Anyone, anyone at all."

Mr. Ballard was adamant that he and Sam were the only two people with a key.

Wes took the phone and told him about the intruder. He assured Mr. Ballard, who had become very upset, that the matter would be investigated. He ended the conversation with the promise that Samantha would not be allowed to stay at the house while he was away.

The two walked outside and around the periphery of the house inspecting the entries, but all were intact with no signs of forced entry. Wes inspected the ground for footprints, but there were none. Upon returning, they found they had locked themselves out: the key was in Sam's handbag and it had been left inside. Sam raised the garage door with the remote control that was in her car. Wes took a small packet from his coat and removed a tiny instrument: it took only a moment for him to pick the lock and open the door from the garage into the hallway.

"Do you think the intruder could have got in that way?" Samantha asked.

"Not the front door. Deadbolts aren't easy to open with one of these things and I doubt if he came through the garage. He probably didn't have a remote."

"But how would he get in?"

"Probably had a key..."

"But Dad said..."

"Come on, Kitten. Let's look again: we may have missed something."

A second and more thorough search of the entire house failed to turn up even the slightest evidence of foul play. Tired of the game, Sam flopped down on the living room sofa. "I'm beginning to think Mrs. Hatch was mistaken," she said. "Maybe he wasn't in the house at all. Maybe he was just..." Samantha jerked forward. "Wes!"

"What? Something missing?"

"Yes! Something is *definitely* missing!" Sam fell to her knees and began to inspect the coffee table. "The table, Wes! Dust is missing. When I was here looking for pictures of Maria, this table was dirty: the glass top was stained with coffee rings. Dad is a terrible housekeeper. I remember thinking how I would clean for him this weekend. The dust and coffee rings are *gone*, Wes! That's what's missing!"

"Maybe your Dad cleaned the table before he left."

"No, he left long before I did and he couldn't have come back. He had to catch a plane."

"Maybe *you* did it without..."

"No, I never had time for that. I had to meet you for lunch, remember?"

She stood up and inspected the room again. The table was the only thing that had been dusted.

"Where does your father keep the cleaning equipment?" Wes asked.

"I don't know. I...Probably the same place as before? Why?"

"Show me."

She took him to the laundry room and opened a cabinet door. He reached in and gently lifted the window cleaner placing the tip of his little finger under the handle. Next to the cleaner was a rag. As he expected, it was wet and smelled like ammonia.

"Why would somebody clean just the coffee table, Wes?"

"I don't know, unless he—or she—was trying to remove evidence. Fingerprints maybe. But it has to be someone that knows your house and where the cleaning equipment is kept. Otherwise, they would have grabbed a towel. I would have noticed a wet towel."

"You suspect Maria again, don't you?"

"She wouldn't have a key. Girlfriend, maybe."

"No, not Dad!"

"How can you be sure? He probably doesn't want you to know about her. Maybe *she* has a key."

Sam was reluctant to agree, but she could think of nothing better. "Okay, maybe Dad has a girlfriend. Why wouldn't he want me to know?"

"Loyalty, embarrassment, respect for your mother. Where are the plastic bags?"

She found them in the kitchen drawer. Wes took two and carefully placed the wet rag and the window cleaner inside. Leaving the items on the coffee table, he said, "Okay, Kitten, now show me where your father might keep current bills."

"You sure don't make things simple, do you? I've been gone five years, you know." Sam walked into the hall and into her father's den. Wes followed.

Mr. Ballard's desk was neatly arranged: two stacks of papers were organized and placed to the right and left of a desk pad. Two drawers were locked, but Wes found what he wanted in a tray on top of the desk: it held envelopes—mostly bills—some unopened. Wes sifted through them and found what he was looking for. From the MasterCard statement, he scribbled the account number onto a slip of paper, then he carried a sealed envelope to the kitchen and turned on the hot water. The steam dampened the seal, he lifted it and took out the contents: the telephone bill.

"Your father makes a lot of calls: some of them to the same party. I want a copy of this. Can I take it with me?"

Sam nodded.

"Then I want you to return it to exactly the same place, Kitten, sealed. I don't want your dad to know I opened it. Okay?"

"Okay, okay. But what are you looking for, Wes?"

"Detectives usually don't know what they're looking for until they find it, my dear."

Baffled and a bit disturbed, Sam turned and opened the refrigerator. "I'm starved. Want a sandwich?"

"Yeah, I'll have one. And coffee, decaf, if you have it. I think my ulcer's coming back."

"Then you'll have milk!"

"Ugh, you remind me of your mother. She was always pushing milk on me. Speaking of your mother, how is she?"

"The same. She doesn't remember me. Her doctor says it's denial, that I look like Cindy and in order to escape from a trauma she can't cope with, she has to deny us both."

"Does she remember your father?"

"No, he used to visit her every week, but I don't think he goes much anymore. It's a long drive, and she doesn't even know who he is. She was catatonic for over a year, you know."

"Yes, I know. It was right after you left for college. I visited her once, but her doctor said it was useless for me to come so I stopped going."

While Sam prepared lunch, Wes made a phone call to the hotel desk clerk where Ballard was staying. "This is Mr. Ballard calling from outside the hotel. I'm a guest there—Room 408. I made a long distance call from my room a few minutes ago. Can you tell me if it went through on my card okay?"

The voice at the other end was polite, but cold. "I'll check, sir." The wait was short. "No, sir, it didn't. It went through our board and will be on your hotel bill. I'm sorry, sir."

"Look, I left the party's number in my suitcase. Could you give it to me? It's important that I call them again right away."

"Oh, I'm sorry, sir, but..."

"Look, I'm going to be in a lot of trouble if I don't catch the guy quick. Just give me the number and save my neck."

"Well...I suppose it would be all right if I can verify your identity. Can you tell me your credit card number?"

Wes held up the paper with Mr. Ballard's MasterCard number and repeated it over the phone. The clerk was satisfied.

"It was 503-555-2724, sir."

"Thank you, you're a doll." Wes hung up, smiling. *Just as I figured: a local number*, he thought as he dialed it. *Now we'll see who Ballard was so anxious to talk to.*

The phone was answered on the first ring. It was a real estate office.

Eleven

Reminding her not to return to her father's house without him, Wes dropped Sam off at her apartment and went straight to the real estate office. It was a small building at the north end of Beaverton. *Probably four or five agents at the most*, he concluded after looking around. While waiting for someone to assist him, he wondered if Ballard has listed his home for sale. No, he decided it was a personal call to someone he knew—and an urgent call at that.

There were only two people in the office—a man and a woman—and both were on the telephone. The woman finally hung up and came over to him.

"I'm doing a little preliminary footwork for a friend," he said. "He's interested in the hills west of the city. Do you have any listings there?"

"I'm sure there must be something. What price range?"

Gordon took a quick guess at the value of the Ballard home and said, "Between six and eight hundred thousand, I suppose."

The agent straightened up with renewed interest and said, "I'll look on the computer."

The woman came back five minutes later with a paper in her hand. "There are several homes in that category, all very nice. May I arrange to show them to you?"

"Are you familiar with the area yourself?"

"No, I'm not, but I'm sure I can..."

He interrupted. "I would like to work with an agent that has been there and knows the area. Do you have one here?"

The woman paused to think. After a moment of disappointment, she said, "Melanie knows the area. She should be back soon. May I have her call you?"

"No, I'll come by later. What time do you expect her?"

"In about an hour. Can you come back then?"

"I'll call her. What's her last name?"

"Taylor. Melanie Taylor."

"Thank you." Gordon turned to leave.

"But your name. I don't have *your* name."

It was too late. He had already gone.

Gordon dropped the window cleaner and cleaning rag off at the lab and headed back to his office at the precinct. He poured over the phone bill he had taken from the Ballard home. Three numbers were called consistently. Picking up the phone on his desk, he touched the intercom button. "Lisa, is the reverse directory at your desk?"

He searched through the book until he found the first number: a stockbroker—and always an early morning call. The second number was a four-one-five area code. *San Francisco. Why would he call there so often?*

The third number confirmed his suspicions. "Taylor! M. Taylor!" he almost shouted. He made a mental note of the hour the calls were made—usually in the evening—and the number of times she had been called: fourteen. He removed a small notebook from his pocket and added her to the list of suspects. Now there were three.

"Gordon, get in here!" Chief O'Malley's voice nearly shattered his eardrum. He put the receiver back in its cradle, rubbed his ear and headed toward the chief's office.

His superior had assumed his usual position when he was angry. Hands clenched together behind his broad back, he was pacing the floor behind his desk. His bushy, gray hair was ruffled from the fingers that had been sifting through it and his glasses were barely hanging from his bulbous, red nose. Unknowing, one might think he was a heavy drinker, but he never touched the stuff. The nose turned red when he got upset.

As the detective entered, the chief glared, picked up a folder from his desk and waved it over his head. "Mrs. Winfield's dog. What have you done to find her dog?"

Gordon was caught off-guard. The case he was on when Sam returned had been put aside and left untouched. He hesitated to answer and the chief continued his outburst.

"It's the Ballard case again, isn't it? It has started all over." He pointed a finger to a chair and shouted, "Sit down!" He plunged into his own chair and leaned forward. Elbows dug into the desk as he linked his fingers together and raised his left eyebrow. "What's going on, Gordon?"

"Chief, I've come up with suspects. Three!"

"Three!"

"That's right, Chief."

"Who are they?"

"I'd rather not say right now."

The chief slammed his fist down and spun around in his chair. Returning it to its position, he blurted out. "And why not?"

"Because you'd have to tell the FBI and there are reasons why I don't want them to know yet."

"But what about the dog?"

"Put someone else on it."

The chief scratched his head and stood up. He walked to the window and looked out, then turned and stared at the detective. "And the FBI? What do I tell them?"

"Bear with me, Chief. Let me work on the case without them for a couple of days. If I don't have something worthwhile by then, I'll give you what I've got and you can turn it over to them."

Reluctantly, he conceded. "Okay. Forty-eight hours. I'll give you forty-eight, no more. Now get outta here."

Gordon left, closing the door behind him. The chief watched him through the interior window as he strode off triumphantly. With mixed emotions and shaking his head, the chief touched a button on his telephone. "Carol, send in Jensen. I hear he's fond of dogs."

Back at his desk, Gordon pulled the notebook from his pocket and opened it. He stared at the three names: *Maria Gonzales Corelli; Anthony Corelli, MD; Melanie Taylor.*

He wished his old partner, Juan Aguila, was still on the force. The two had worked well together for four years before Juan got shot and was retired disabled. What one could not come up with, the other did: except for the Cindy Ballard case when they got nowhere. But now he had something worthwhile: something they could both work on. It helped to bounce your ideas off someone, to talk out loud. There was Samantha, but he didn't want her to know about her father yet—and Melanie Taylor. Juan had always been a good sounding board and a good thinker. He decided to pay Juan a visit.

The lettering on the door was done in gold leaf and it said, *Juan Aguila, Carter Finley, Private Investigators.* Aguila was sitting at his desk, arguing with someone on the phone when Gordon entered. He glanced up.

"I'll call you back later, Tom. In the meantime, think about it." He hung up and rushed to greet him. "Wes Gordon, you old fool! It's about time you came around." The two embraced.

"You have a partner, I see. How long?"

"Six months. I gave up waiting for you. Have a chair." Aguila slugged him in the shoulder and pulled up a chair for himself as well.

"You look great! How's the leg?"

"Still hanging in there. I get around. What's new?"

"Samantha. She's back and wants me to reopen the case."

"You gonna do it?"

"I've got some leads, Juan. New evidence we never came across before. They're hot." Gordon told his old buddy about Maria and the other suspects, then leaned back. "What do you think?"

"I think you're onto something, that's what I think."

"Will you help me?"

"I'm on a case right now. But I can give it some time. What do you want me to do?"

"I need you to check out the Corellis. Trace their history, find out what they're doing, how they're fixed financially, all that."

"What makes you think they're still together?"

"Maybe they're not. If they've split up, you've got twice as much work to do. In the meantime, I'm going to look into some bank records and phone bills—and Melanie Taylor."

Twelve

It was too late to expect cooperation from the phone company or the banks—that would have to wait until Monday—but the real estate agent would be easy to track down. Her address was in the reverse directory.

Gordon pressed hard on the gas pedal and headed north on Interstate Five, then to Willamette Boulevard.

Her house overlooked the river: it was old and modest, but well kept. He parked fifty feet away, across the street and waited. Forty minutes later, a silver Toyota pulled into the driveway. A shapely but small-boned woman with blonde hair and who appeared to be in her late thirties got out. Without effort, she lifted the garage door, got back into her car and drove in. The door was closed from the inside.

Planning on spending the evening at home, he thought, as he watched her image through the living room window from his vantage point. Then, as dusk turned to dark, she closed the drapes. He opened his car door and got out.

Down the street a car door slammed and the car pulled away. No one else seemed to be around. He crossed the street and with cat-like strides walked alongside the blonde woman's house and to the back. He peered through an opening in the bedroom window drapes and saw her again. She was placing an article of clothing in a suitcase. *Won't be gone long*, he thought. *The suitcase is small.* It was his guess that she would make a phone call before leaving the house.

Gordon returned to his car and opened the trunk lid. Surveillance equipment was kept in a case, all neatly organized and ready for use. He removed a small black box and then reconsidered. Putting a tap on her phone line and recording a conversation was not only illegal, but it would not hold up in court if it ever got that far. He put the black box back in its place and decided to use a shotgun mike. He would only be able to hear her side of the conversation, but he could listen from his car. Gently, he closed the trunk lid and with the shotgun mike in hand, he slipped back inside the car. He set up and activated the mike, then waited. Ten minutes later he heard her dial a number. Then....

"I've written it down, Jim. Room 408 at the Edgemont. I can be there by midnight. My plane leaves at ten-twenty."

There was a pause.

"Yes, I got the file. It was in your desk where you said. I have it right here.

Another pause.

"Five thousand. It's in my suitcase. See you later, Sugar."

Gordon turned off the mike, laid it on the passenger seat and took the notebook from his pocket. Under the name *Melanie Taylor*, he added two words: *James Ballard.*

Gordon picked up a pizza and headed home. It took over an hour to trace down Aguila, but he finally found him and talked him into flying to Reno.

"I'll pick up the bill," he said. "It'll be a nice vacation."

"Tailing was never a vacation, but I'll do it. When does the plane leave?"

"In forty minutes. Can you make it? I've already booked reservations and your room at the Edgemont. He's in room 408, you're across the hall. Anything yet on the Corellis?"

"Nothing exciting. I'll fill you in later. Gotta catch a plane."

Samantha opened the living room drapes, fluffed the pillows on the secondhand sofa she had been given and flopped down. She looked around the room and thought about new wallpaper. Deciding against it, she recalled the episode at her father's house and winced at the thought of a stranger invading it. She thought about Wes. Being with him again was exhausting and she had a headache. She grabbed the remote control and switched on the TV, then switched it off again. She tried to sleep, but sleep would not come.

She thought about Bubbles and was sorry she had died. The little dog had always sensed when the twins were upset and gave them comfort. *Maybe I should get a dog,* she thought. *No, I'm gone too much. Maybe a cat.*

She decided to clean the apartment: dust was collecting on the furniture. Then she remembered her father's house needed cleaning even more. *Tomorrow,* she thought, ignoring Wes's warning.

As she ran the vacuum, she became disturbed over his intrusion into her father's personal papers. Why didn't she stop him? Was it really necessary to go through his bills? Why did he want a copy of her father's phone bill? The more she thought about it, the angrier she became. Did he suspect her father? Of what? Of having a girlfriend? It was none of his business. Her mother had been gone for ten years; her father was still virile and healthy. *He has as much right to happiness as anyone. A girlfriend? More power to him; I would like to meet her.*

Samantha turned off the vacuum and put it back in the closet.

As she was dusting the bedroom, she noticed the little box sitting open on top of the dresser. *The letter: it's still in my handbag!* She had decided not to give it to Wes: the time was not right. And the threat was still hanging over her head. Could the person who sent it know she was back? Could he—or she—be watching her? *It's been five years and nothing has happened.*

It was probably from a prankster having a field day and I took it too seriously.

Exhausted, Sam fell onto the bed, convinced the letter was old and useless. Nothing had come from it, threats had never been carried out. As her eyes closed, she made the decision that tomorrow she would return it to the box where it had been kept for five years. *Tomorrow...Maybe tomorrow I'll destroy it...*

The dream was nightmarish. Sam was but a tiny speck of a girl slashing at a huge sheet of paper with a baseball bat. The paper had taken on humanistic qualities and was fighting back. It towered over her like an enormous blanket trying to smother her. There were words printed on the paper that she couldn't understand—they seemed to be in a foreign language—but the *O's* stood out, and from them oozed black ink that spilled on her each time she struck at it with the bat.

Sam slashed out with her arms. The motion woke her from the nightmare and she sat up frightened and confused. *The letter! I must destroy the letter now!* She pulled herself from the bed and started searching for her handbag. She found it on the kitchen table. Nervous and fumbling, she dropped it on the floor. It opened: her lipstick rolled out and under the refrigerator. Grabbing the bag up, she looked inside. The letter was gone!

Thirteen

The sun had just come up when the phone rang. Gordon crawled out of bed. It was Aguila calling from Reno.

"They spent most of the night at the tables, then went to his room. They've been in there for two hours. Want me to stick with it?"

"Yeah, hang around. Any idea why the money?"

"My guess is for the tables. They blew a lot."

"Cash any checks?"

"Nope, used cash. I'd guess they went through a thou. I'll call you later." Aguila hung up.

It was 10:15 that evening when Aguila arrived at Gordon's apartment. The two huddled over the small table in the center of the kitchen. Hot coffee was beginning to perk in the coffeemaker and the microwave signaled the TV dinners were ready. Both were ignored.

"I stuck with 'em most of the day. He was in a meeting all morning. She gambled, did a little drinking at a bar, then back to the tables. They had lunch, gambled some more, then spent the rest of the day in his room. I came back with her on the plane. He stayed—another meeting tomorrow. She never saw me tailing her."

"Good work. What did you find out about the Corellis?"

"He's a psychiatrist, licensed in both Washington and Oregon and has a clean record in both states. His practice is in the Penwick Building."

"Penwick? Must be doing okay to afford Penwick. Know where he lives? Are they still married?"

"As far as I know. Live in Hillsboro—the better part. I drove past the house: it's plush. It was too late to get more. Want me to stake 'em out?"

"Tomorrow. Got time?"

Aguila glanced at the microwave. "I'll squeeze it in. What did *you* come up with?"

"Not a lot. Spent the day going through more records and making useless phone calls. It was wasted time." Gordon stood up and reached for the coffee. He poured two cups, slung the TV dinners on the table and handed Aguila a fork.

Aguila scraped the plastic container clean and said, "Is this all you've got to eat? Do you always eat this stuff?"

"Keeps my weight down."

"Heck, it's not enough to make a fly fat."

"I'll make you a sandwich. Peanut butter?"

"No thanks."

"What do you think of Ballard?" Gordon asked.

"Not surprised."

"What do you mean, not surprised?"

"He's okay, I guess. Bet he cheated on his wife before."

"Before what?"

"Before she was committed. Wake up, man. Didn't you ever notice how he treated her?"

"He respected her."

"Nah, he faked it. I don't think he loved her."

Gordon threw the empty dinner containers in the garbage and wiped off the table. He poured more coffee and sat down again, then stood, dumped his own coffee in the sink and poured himself a glass of milk from the refrigerator.

"Ulcer acting up again, huh?"

Gordon ignored the question. Stroking his chin, he said, "How come you never mentioned it before?"

"Never mentioned what before?"

"Ballard. That you didn't like him."

"Never had a reason to."

Gordon remained silent—thinking.

Aguila let it simmer a while then said, "You don't suspect Ballard. What would be his motive?"

"Haven't figured that one out yet."

Aguila scoffed. "Like I said, I never liked the guy, but kidnap his own daughter? Then take the ransom money from his own bank? Doesn't add up."

"You're probably right."

"He could have been convicted, you know? If the money had been picked up. He was lucky to get off and keep his job." Aguila stood up and poured himself another cup.

"The board felt sorry for him. Said he left a note that he'd sign loan papers later. They didn't want to press charges." He paused. "Juan, you think he might have planned the whole thing, even down to the fire? Maybe he intended to put the money back before...No, forget it. Dumb idea."

"You sure you're not grasping at straws? For a conviction?"

Gordon resented the remark. "What do you take me for? You think I'd..." He was about to blow, but decided Aguila was right. "Yeah, I thought I had something, but I guess it's just a love affair—to be expected, I suppose. After all, his wife's been out to lunch for ten years now."

Aguila sat down again. "Now the Corellis, that's another matter. You might have something there, but give me a motive."

"Money. *That* bank account was zilch just a few months earlier, but he probably had another account somewhere so I've discounted that idea. But the account in question: it grew to the tune of twenty-five hundred a month."

"How do you know?"

"Got the bank statements. That's how I knew she married Corelli."

"Bribery?" suggested Aguila.

"Maybe. Or a payoff—in advance."

"Or blackmail." Aguila squinted and stood. "No, Wes, none of that makes sense. Twenty-five hundred? Could have been for her to pay the household bills."

"That's possible."

"Then why the curiosity?"

"Because the deposits were monthly—four months only. And they stopped after Cindy was abducted."

Aguila scratched his head and sat down again. "Was it cash?"

"Don't know yet. Won't know till Monday when the banks open."

"Where do you think the money came from?"

"If it was cash, we'll never know, will we?"

Aguila stood up. "I'm going home: it's midnight."

Gordon followed him to the door, thanked him for the help and said he'd talk to him tomorrow. He closed the door and turned out the living room lamp. Standing at the window looking out at the city lights, he repeated again the question he had asked himself so many times. *Who would kidnap Cindy? Was it some nut after the money, then botched the job, or was it someone the family knew? And why?*

As he closed the drapes, his thoughts returned to Ballard and Melanie Taylor. He decided to leave their names on the list.

Fourteen

Sam was frantic. The letter must be found. She searched her apartment and her car; she called La Casita and asked if it had been turned in. She remembered her bag had fallen open in Wes's car and she worried that it might be there. She prayed that he would not discover it.

She returned to her father's house and searched, but the letter seemed to have vanished into thin air. Weary and defeated, she decided to remain the night. She had promised Wes she would not go there without him, but she had to find the letter. He would be angry, but she didn't care. She felt safe in her childhood home; it was good to be there with old memories — without her father. And the house needed cleaning.

She envisioned her mother returning and seeing it in its present condition. *She'll never return*, she thought as she dusted the furniture and mopped the floors. But she was impelled by a force she could not understand. Until it happened.

While polishing the mirror over the dresser in her former bedroom, Cindy's voice called out to her.

She spun around, but there was no one there. Yet, as on previous occasions, she could feel her sister's presence. She could hear her speaking, calling out to her.

Hurry, Samantha, hurry, before it's too late. We need you. Hurry!

"Cindy!" Sam called out. "Cindy, what is it? Where are you?"

There was no response. Tears forming, she pleaded, "Cindy, don't go away. Where are you? What is it?"

"*Hurry, Sam, hurry!*"

Again Sam called out to her sister, but there was no answer and the sensation began to fade.

Why did Cindy say *we,* she wondered. Who, beside herself, was she referring to? Confused and bewildered, she slid to the floor. She sat there for a moment, agonizing and straining to hold back the tears. Then she stood and took control of her emotions. Leaning on the dresser, she stared into the mirror and calmly said, "Cindy, I know you are trying to tell me something. You are with someone. Are you both in danger? Who is with you?"

There was no answer.

For a long time she remained fixed, sifting through the past, assessing the present and fearing the future. Was she wasting her time? Had Wes been right all these years? Were the premonitions, the voices, merely her imagination rising out of desire, out of hope? She probed her feelings and began to doubt her own motives. For the first time in her life she said it and she said it aloud. It was as if she were trying on a new dress to see if it would fit.

"Cindy is dead."

But it didn't fit and she knew it was not true.

She considered visiting a psychiatrist. *Why? I'm a normal and well-adjusted person.* Then for a moment, she wondered about her sanity and its preservation. And she thought about her mother. But only for a moment.

The thought of seeking out a medium passed through her mind, but she dismissed it. She knew little about mediums, but she reasoned that if they had such powers, it was for communicating with the dead and Cindy was not dead.

She thought about hypnosis to bring out the past, then she scolded herself: the past was vivid in her mind.

She stood up, walked to the window and looked out at the backyard. While she was reminiscing, a tiny cyclone gathered together a nest of dried maple leaves and forced them to dance. As they spun around and around, Sam hummed the tune *Here We Go 'Round the Mulberry Bush* until the wind tired of the game and released the little red leaves from its grasp.

The rusty swing set below caught her attention. One swing was wrapped around the pole, the wooden seat tapping out a message to be freed.

As she stood there counting the taps, she knew she had to free Cindy.

Then, for the first time, she felt her mother sought freedom as well.

Without hesitation and with the lost letter erased from her mind, Samantha decided it was time to visit her mother. *Tomorrow*, she thought. *Tomorrow morning I'll wash the windows, then I'll go see mother.*

Fifteen

Anthony Corelli, M.D., pulled into the parking lot behind the building and looked up at the second floor window just above him. The drapes were still closed. *She must be sleeping*, he thought as he started to enter the back door. He decided to walk across the lawn and look out over the valley first. He didn't want to see her yet.

The grass was still damp from the light rain that had fallen during the night and the trees glistened as the early morning sun cast its light on their wet needles. It was peaceful here: a perfect place for the mentally ill.

They bought the ten acres and the eighty-year-old mansion long before they could afford it, but it was too perfect to let slip by at such a reasonable price. He had been approached by his colleague, Rudy Fischer, shortly after they finished their residency. Fischer's parents had left him a substantial inheritance, more than enough for the down payment, but he wanted Corelli to join him in the venture. Corelli agreed and took out a loan for his share, a small share.

Jointly, they obtained another loan and began the renovation. A year later, and just before Corelli and Maria Gonzales were married, they opened *Serenity-In-The-Hills*. Corelli's and Fischer's dream had come true.

The newlyweds splurged on a honeymoon in Hawaii, then returned to Portland to buy a condo in the West hills. They overspent, but Corelli's practice was already stabilizing and they felt they could afford it. Fischer was patient and made the payments on the business loans himself for a while. *You'll be doing your share soon enough*, Fischer said. But it took longer than he hoped.

Corelli turned and looked back at the home that had been a shelter for the mentally disturbed for thirteen years now. He had been in partnership with Fischer during the first few years, but eventually he and Maria had other plans and he pulled out staying on as a paid employee to treat a few selected patients. Carla Ballard was one of them.

Initially, Fischer lived in the small guesthouse behind the eight-bedroom mansion, then he built a new home a few miles away for himself and *his* bride-to-be.

The wedding was called off. She decided his profession was too demanding and at times depressing and ran off with an airline pilot. Fischer sold the home he built for her at a fair profit and eventually adjusted to the disappointment, but never again dated a woman. He preferred to devote his time to his patients and *Serenity*.

Corelli took one last look at the valley and the distant highway with its steady line of cars: city folk on their way to the coast. He wanted to be among them. It was Sunday. He would rather spend the day at their beach house, but Maria had awakened with another headache and Fischer had called him during the night. Mrs. Ballard was not doing well: she demanded to see him.

Corelli expanded his lungs with the fresh morning air, then exhaled forcefully and headed back to the mansion. He would have to see her. He wished he had never let Maria talk him into getting involved, but he loved his wife and it seemed to be a solution to a problem. Never did he dream it would become an eleven-year nightmare.

He ascended the back stairs and turned down the hall toward her room. The maid was stuffing laundry in a bag and mumbling something about an old man that soiled his sheets just to give her more work. When she saw him, she stopped.

"Doctor Corelli! I didn't know you would be here today. Is Doctor Fischer leaving?"

"No, I just stopped in to see Mrs. Ballard. I hear she has been rather unruly this past week."

"I wouldn't know, Doctor. I just clean her room. She seems fine when I'm here."

The maid watched the tall, slender man enter Room 24 and paused to fantasize a moment. He seemed particularly handsome this morning, but not as friendly as usual. *He looks worried.* She shrugged her shoulders and went about her work. *Not my concern*, she thought. *I just clean the rooms and do the laundry. I'm not to ask questions.*

The doctor stood over the woman's bed. She appeared to be sleeping, but when he turned to walk away, she spoke. "You haven't been in to see me, Doctor. Don't you care about me anymore?"

Corelli paused, then looked back at her. She had not moved. The blanket was still pulled over her head. *How did she know I was here?* He thought. *They have a sixth sense, these people, and they comprehend more than we think.* He walked back to the bed and pulled down the cover. "I've been busy, and they said you were doing fine."

Mrs. Ballard sat up in bed. Her golden tresses were interspersed with streaks of gray and tiny lines around her eyes and lips belied her otherwise youthful appearance. Her nightgown dropped from her left shoulder and she quickly pulled it up again.

The doctor sat on the edge of her bed and touched her hand. "What is it you want, my dear?" he asked.

"I want to go home. They won't let me go home."

Wesley Gordon looked into the mirror and rubbed his chin. *Sandpaper, coarse sandpaper*, he thought. But it was Sunday: he always felt that men should not have to shave on Sunday. Taking a deep breath, he puffed up his chest, flexed his biceps and reached for the shaving cream.

As he stroked his jaw with the tiny blade, he mulled over the bits of information he had stored in his head. Mentally, he organized them into some form of logical sequence and recited the list to his mirrored image.

"Maria Gonzales. Babysat four-and-a-half years. Faithful, loved the kids. Maybe. Maybe not. Got fired because she disobeyed orders: took twins to her house. Resentful? Wanted to get even? No, wanted the kid: partial to Cindy. Missed her. No, got married: could have had her own. Maybe not. Needed money? Maybe."

He shifted the blade to the other side of his face and continued with his list.

"Anthony Corelli. A doctor. Doctor's don't need money. Not true, not today. Could have been in trouble. Debts, maybe. New practice? New wife. New home? When did he buy the home in Hillsboro?" He made a mental note to check it out, washed the cream off his face and reached for the towel. While drying himself, he continued with his list.

"James Ballard. Father. Successful, devoted to family. Loyal to wife? Maybe not." He threw the towel at the mirror and shouted. "But that's not a reason to kidnap your own kid! It's not a reason. Motive! I need a motive!"

He stomped into the bedroom and yanked the window shade down, letting it fly up. Standing in his shorts and looking out at the city, he yelled. "Where are you, Cindy? Where are you? Are you dead or alive? Who did this to you? And to Sam?" More calmly, he added, "And to your mother?" Then he remembered the day Mrs. Ballard was taken away.

Carla Ballard took one last look at her home before stepping into the car. Her husband opened the trunk and put her suitcase inside, walked to the driver's side and got in. Wesley Gordon closed Carla's door, waved good-bye and returned to the porch where Samantha was waiting.

She was only fourteen, but she understood. Her mother was being admitted to a special hospital for treatment of her severe depression. She had not wanted to leave her home, but Mr. Ballard had insisted. She finally agreed on condition that she would be permitted to visit the hospital first and pass approval. They had inspected three before she made her choice.

"Will she come back, Wesley?" Sam asked.

"Sure she will, Kitten. The doctors will help her with her illness. They'll help her forget about Cindy so she can think about you, then you'll be able to be a family again."

"No!" Sam shouted. "Not until Cindy comes back. We'll never be a family till you find Cindy."

As Gordon watched a freighter inch it's way down the Willamette, he regretted telling Sam her mother would come back someday. He could still see the expression on Mrs. Ballard's face as she climbed into the car and left her home. Now, looking back, he recalled the expression was one of hopelessness and defeat, not denial. The family doctor said it was denial that made her ignore Samantha. It was a defense mechanism against something she couldn't accept. And he recommended a psychiatrist.

Something didn't add up. He decided it was time to visit Carla Ballard again—and her shrink. What was his name? Fischer. Doctor Rudy Fischer.

He thought about inviting Samantha to take the trip to the mountains where *Serenity-In-the-Hills* was located, then perhaps go on to the coast for the day, but decided better of it. There was too much to do to waste time walking the beach, and he didn't want his relationship with Sam to become personal again.

As he turned off Highway 26 and onto the road that led to *Serenity*, he thought about James Ballard. Juan's theory that he had not been faithful to his wife prior to the kidnapping was absurd. Or was it? Perhaps he had become too close to the family, too close to the forest to see the trees. But even if he had cheated on his wife, how could that have anything to do with the kidnapping? He decided to remove the twins' father from his list of suspects. For him to be having an affair now was to be expected: his wife was living in another world, one that did not include him. Any healthy man would have done the same.

Driving through the pines and along the ridge that overlooked the valley gave him a sense of distance from the Ballard family. He opened the window, filled his lungs with the crisp air and lightened his foot on the gas pedal. It was a beautiful day and he decided to take his time and enjoy the drive. At a turnout, he stopped to admire the view and failed to notice the car coming down the hill driven by a tall, slender man named Anthony Corelli.

Sixteen

It had been nearly five years since Gordon was there. The mansion had been painted a delicate pink with white trim. It had a restful appearance, but the new wrought iron fence surrounding the property suggested inhospitality. He drove to the gate that barred his entry, reached out the window and pressed the button that activated the intercom. A husky voice asked him to identify himself.

"Detective Wesley Gordon with the Portland Police, ma'am. I would like to speak with Doctor Fischer about Mrs. Ballard."

"One moment please." The intercom remained silent for nearly two minutes and then finally came to life. "Hold your badge up to the camera, please."

Gordon obeyed, the gate opened and he drove through.

He remembered the grounds well. The shrubs and trees had grown considerably since he last visited Carla Ballard, and two more small buildings had been added. Unconsciously, he nodded as he thought of the man who had originally built the mansion eighty-some years earlier. *Charles VanOrden, the Third, would be pleased,* he thought. *It looks good.*

VanOrden had been one of the first shipping magnates to make big money in the Portland area. He built the mansion after he made his second million as a peace offering for the wife who rarely saw him. She accepted it graciously. So graciously she caused him to go into bankruptcy with her lavish and frequent purchases of furnishings and art goods from all over the world, and then with the spectacular balls and dinners she held to show them off. VanOrden died of a broken heart—they say—when he found he was not only stripped of his wealth but also of his wife when she committed suicide. It was rumored that the mansion was haunted by the VanOrden ghosts, and consequently was sold six times over the ensuing years. Doctor Fischer apparently put the VanOrdens to rest when he turned it into a successful home for the mentally disturbed, although one might expect such a place to be the perfect playground for a poltergeist.

Gordon drove his car into the lot marked *Visitors Parking*, got out and walked the distance to the massive stairway that led to the entrance of the mansion. The gigantic, double doors had been changed. He remembered them as having sparkling crystal oval windows: now the doors had no windows at all. Impressive, but solid and uninviting. He touched the doorbell. Again, the husky voice spoke to him.

"Detective Gordon?"

"Yes, ma'am—sir." Was it a man or a woman's voice?

"You may enter."

He heard a click and he pulled the door open.

The entry of the mansion had been altered from its original French decor and was now contemporary and uninteresting. To the left, a small office had been added. It marred the impressiveness of what was once a grand entry, but Gordon understood it's necessity.

The receptionist opened a glass window. She was short, had delicate features and ebony black skin. When she spoke, Gordon was taken back. Her voice was the same husky voice he had heard over the intercom. It didn't match her appearance.

"May I see your badge, Detective?"

He showed the badge again.

"Doctor Fischer will be with you in a moment. Please have a seat over there."

He walked across the entry to a pair of high-backed chairs and sat down. Five minutes later a short, stocky man with carrot-red hair and squinty, green eyes entered the room. Hand extended, he walked toward Gordon.

The doctor's hand was soft and flabby and he was quick to loosen the firm grip of the detective. "Did you enjoy the ride up, Mister.... What did you say your name is?"

"Gordon. Detective Gordon with the Portland Police. The ride was pleasant. You're lucky to live here."

"Yes, I am, but how did you know I live here?"

Gordon shifted his weight. "You probably don't remember me. It was I who made a thorough investigation of this place—and you—ten years ago, just prior to Mrs. Ballard's admission. Mr. Ballard wanted to admit her to one closer to the city, but Carla insisted on your place."

"Yes, I remember you now. You, if I'm not mistaken, are the officer who investigated the Ballard case. You were quite tenacious."

Gordon looked down at his feet; then, with a tone of renewed courage said, "You're not mistaken, Doctor. I tried, but failed."

"Don't blame yourself, young man. If I recall correctly, the FBI put forth great effort and failed as well. No one can succeed in changing what cannot be changed. But let's move to more comfortable quarters. You didn't come to talk about yourself, I suspect."

The psychiatrist turned and gestured toward his office.

The room was spacious and lavishly furnished. What was spared in decorating the entry was spent a hundred-fold in Fischer's private domain. One corner held an enormous mahogany desk and a dark red, leather chair trimmed in wood that matched the desk perfectly. Both were obviously antiques. Behind was a ceiling-to-floor bookcase that occupied the entire wall. Gordon walked over to it and perused the titles of the books. It was filled with volumes written on the subjects of psychiatry and psychology. There was a miscellany of unrelated titles, one of which caught his eye: *Powders, Solutions and Herbs: Toxic and Deadly.* At the opposite side of the room there was an easy chair, contemporary in style, but again in dark red leather, and a matching couch.

"Have a seat, Detective." The doctor waved his hand toward the couch and without removing his eyes from Gordon, took a seat in the easy chair.

"Here? I hope you're not thinking of psychoanalyzing me," he said, sitting erectly on the edge of the couch.

The doctor chuckled briefly and said, "Only if you request it. Now, what is your question? About Mrs. Ballard, I assume."

"Yes. How is she doing, Doctor? Is there any hope for her recovery?"

"Her progress has been very slow, but we've had some success. She hasn't been catatonic for over two years now."

"I know about her depression. What else?"

"Depression, and at times, paranoia."

"She's paranoid? What's she afraid of?"

"Anything and everyone: it comes and goes. Depression can evolve into a psychosis, you know, which is what has happened in her case. Some people slip into schizophrenia, paranoia or both. Others become manic-depressive. They can all be suicidal. It all depends on the cause of the illness and their reaction to it."

"Has she been suicidal?"

"Oh, yes, many times. We have to watch her very closely."

"What brought it on?"

"Losing a child, of course. Quite obvious, and not too uncommon."

Gordon paused to think, then went on. "Could an unhappy marriage do this to her?"

"I wasn't aware she had an unhappy marriage. Mr. Ballard has always been attentive. He insists on the best of care for her, money being no object."

"Hmm, yes, but that didn't answer the question."

"To answer the question, yes, it could."

"Do you think Mrs. Ballard will ever go home?"

The doctor shifted his position and hesitated to answer. "Uh, possibly, someday, if Mr. Ballard requests it."

His response was unexpected. "What do you mean—if Mr. Ballard requests it?"

"Well, as I understand it...that is..." The doctor stood and nervously walked to the window. "Mrs. Ballard is very ill. Mr. Ballard recognizes the fact that he is totally unequipped to deal with her problem at home. He has asked that we keep her here until she is cured."

Gordon stood and followed the doctor to the window. "Are you telling me she could be treated at home?"

The doctor continued to look out the window. "No, not necessarily. Well, that is..."

It was clear the doctor was becoming uneasy. The detective grabbed him by the arm and forced a face-to-face confrontation. "Doctor Fischer, it appears that Mrs. Ballard may be hospitalized for reasons other than purely for treatment. Has she ever asked to go home?"

"Not to my knowledge."

"What do you mean, not to your knowledge. She's your patient isn't she? Do you have other doctors here?"

The doctor yanked his arm from the detective's grasp. "Sergeant Gordon, I don't like your accusation."

"It's Lieutenant. And I don't like your evasiveness."

"I think this discussion is ended. Without Mr. Ballard's release, I am unable to give you further information concerning his wife's condition. I have told you too much already."

The doctor walked to his desk, pressed a button beside the phone and spoke. "Jessie, Lieutenant Gordon will be leaving now."

"Just a minute," responded Gordon. "I think I would like to see Mrs. Ballard."

"You'll have to make an appointment for that. We never allow visitors to our patients without an appointment."

"Why not? Do you have something to hide?"

"As I said, our discussion is ended."

At that moment, the husky-voiced receptionist entered the office and held the door open for the detective to exit. The doctor escaped without further word through another door.

"This way, Detective Gordon," she said firmly as she grabbed his arm in a vise-like grip and led him out.

I'll bet she knows karate, he thought as he glared back at her.

Walking across the parking lot to his car, he caught a glimpse of a young woman off in the distance. She was dressed in slacks and sweatshirt and had a scarf tied around her head. She had just removed a large box from the backseat of her car and was struggling to balance its weight. The box concealed her face until she shifted it to her left. Gordon was stunned at what he saw. He reached into the backseat for his binoculars, but they were not there. When he turned to look again, she had disappeared, but he swore she was the image of Samantha.

Seventeen

Gordon drove through the open gate knowing Husky Voice would be watching: it closed promptly after he passed through. He parked under the trees at a turnout a quarter-of-a-mile down the road. He found his binoculars under the passenger's seat, slid from the car and started weaving his way up the hillside toward the fence.

The sun's rays failed to find their way through the tall, dense trees, and the privation of warmth had prevented the ground from drying. The fallen pine needles on the slippery earth made it difficult to keep his footing and he slipped and rolled twenty feet before he stopped. He felt for his weapon: it was still in its holster, but he had dropped the binoculars. He climbed back to the spot where he had fallen: the binoculars were there.

This time, he proceeded more gingerly until he came to the fence. Following it, he worked his way toward the back of the property. By the time he reached a place where he could watch for the girl with the box, he had been gone nearly half an hour. He expected barking dogs, but there were none. He waited. He saw no one. Patiently, he remained fixed and surveyed the grounds.

His shoes were damp and his feet were cold. After observing for another twenty minutes, he decided to go back to the car. *My imagination*, he thought. *Can't be Cindy. She's dead.*

But as he drove back to Portland, he kept seeing the girl with the box.

"Good heavens, Gordon! Where have you been? You look like you've been rolling in the mud with the pigs." Juan Aguila was just leaving the apartment building as Gordon got out of his car.

"Been to church," he answered facetiously, glancing down at his pants. He brushed off some dried earth and pine needles, checked his shoes and started up the steps.

"We've been trying to locate you. Don't you answer your pager anymore? Where's your cell phone?"

"I was out of the car; left them in it. Come on up and I'll fill you in."

Aguila grabbed him by the arm. "Hold it, Wes. I've…" The detective hesitated. "I've got some bad news." Again, he paused, then went on. "They think they've found Cindy."

Gordon stopped short on the first step, turned and blurted, "Cindy? They've found Cindy?"

"They're not sure yet, but it's not good, Wes. Let's go up and I'll give you the scoop."

"Tell me now!" He grabbed the PI by the shoulder and gave him a shake.

"Take it easy, man." He looked around for observers: there was no one. "All right, here it is. A body's been dug up. The West hills, not far from where we found the car. A girl, about twelve or thirteen."

"Buried? How long was she there?"

"It's a guess at this point, but from the decomposition, they think ten or more years. I'm sorry, Wes, really sorry."

Gordon spun around on his heel and writhed. Sitting on the step, he buried his face in his hands to absorb the awful news. And then he stood again. He shoved his hands in his pockets and, looking up at the sky, said, "How'd you know?"

"I went over to the precinct looking for you. They'd just gotten the call. O'Malley let me go along."

"When?"

"Couple of hours ago. Some kids were looking for their ball. Their dog started digging. She wasn't very deep."

"You saw her?"

"Yeah."

"You think it's Cindy?"

"How would I know? There's not much left."

Again Gordon writhed and squirmed. "What am I going to tell Sam, Juan? Does she know yet? Has the media got it?"

"I'm afraid so. But they've promised to sit on it till O'Malley gives 'em the go."

Gordon was in pain. It was as if his own sister had just been found murdered. Samantha had convinced him that Cindy was still alive, he had just seen someone at *Serenity* that lifted his hopes, and now everything was quashed.

Aguila took him by the arm and attempted to lead him into the building. "Let's go up, Wes."

"No, I want to find Sam." Then, with renewed confidence, he said, "Maybe it's not Cindy. Where have they got her?"

"By now? Forensics, I suppose. Come on, I'll take you."

The forensic anthropologist had not yet arrived, but a deputy led them to the stretcher where the remains lay. Ordinarily, the medical examiner would inspect a fresh body, but this was not the typical find. A consultant would be brought in, someone with specialized training in the field.

Gordon lifted the drape. He'd been with the force sixteen years: he knew what to expect. Under the usual circumstances, he would have taken it lightly, but this case was different. He almost expected to see Cindy lying there intact, but there was nothing but bones, hair, nails and a small amount of decomposed fabric.

The deputy seemed to read his mind. "Polyester underwear," he volunteered. "The outer clothing must have been cotton. There were no shoes."

"Female?" Gordon asked, turning away.

"Most likely—twelve, maybe thirteen."

Gordon swallowed the lump in his throat. "Any idea how she died?"

"Nothing obvious. Dr. Kramer will be here shortly to start on her."

"Keep this from the press, will you?"

"Already got orders. No one gets in, nothing gets out—till we get the okay."

Gordon walked away. Aguila followed behind, keeping his distance. He noticed the tears in Gordon's eyes and he knew he needed to be alone. Cops weren't supposed to cry.

Aguila took him back to his apartment. He wanted to be alone, to get in his car and drive, to go to Sam. Maybe she didn't know yet. She wasn't scheduled to work today and if the reporters were keeping the lid on it, she wouldn't know. He had to keep the information from her until they knew for sure.

Eighteen

Gordon pulled up in front of the Ballard home. Sam's car was not there. "Maybe in the garage," he mumbled. He turned the wheels into the curb and set the brake. Hoping, yet fearing she would be there, he hesitated getting out: he didn't want to tell her. He had called her apartment earlier, but there was no answer. The operator at KSG-TV said she had not been in, nor was she scheduled to work until Monday. *Maybe church*, he thought. And hoped.

The news of the decomposed body had leaked out. It was on every radio station he had listened to. Television would have it as well.

"Cursed media!" he bellowed as he leaped from the car. Without looking up, he blurted, "God, don't let her have the radio on! Or the TV!"

He sprung up the steps to the front door and rang the bell. He waited for a moment and rang again. There was no answer.

A voice came from across the street: it was Mrs. Hatch.

"You just missed her, Wes," she shouted.

He walked across to meet her. "Do you know where she went?"

"Church maybe. She was all dressed up, even wore a hat. She spent the night here, then left after washing the windows."

"Windows?"

"She did the living room window an hour ago."

Wes thanked her for the information and silently thanked God for a snoopy neighbor, although he still didn't know where

Sam was headed or if she had heard the news yet. But he was sure she would turn the radio on while driving.

He returned to his car and sat there not knowing what to do next. Mrs. Hatch watched from across the street. He became uncomfortable and started the engine. She returned to her house and he eased away, uncertain about his destination.

If she knows about Cindy...No, it can't be Cindy. It won't be Cindy!

Again, he cursed the media for suggesting that the remains dug up that morning might be Sam's twin sister. He decided to return to the forensics lab. He would call her apartment from there.

Samantha headed west on Highway 26. She hoped she would be able to remember the turn-off that took her north into the mountains. It had been too long.

She wondered why her father discouraged her from visiting her mother the last time she had come home. *She won't remember you, Sam. She doesn't even remember me. The doctor says visitors upset her and only hinder her progress.*

She switched on the radio and punched the buttons past music and talk shows, searching for news. *It would take her mind off Cindy*, she thought. The last button was the voice of Hector Bradley, one of her favorite newscasters.

....but a determination has not yet been made as to the identity of the body. Stay tuned and we will bring you further news as it develops. Now for this message.

The turn-off was coming up. Bored with the commercials, but delighted with the beauty of the scenery, Sam switched off the radio and rolled down the window. The cool, fresh air filled her lungs and she felt renewed and alive. She looked forward to seeing her mother again.

At the gate, she pressed the button beneath the intercom and a husky voice buried in static answered. She responded with her name and a request to visit Mrs. Carla Ballard.

"Sorry, ma'am, but visitors are not allowed without making an appointment first."

"Then I'll make an appointment—right now."

"Sorry, but you have to phone ahead. Go home and call us; maybe we can arrange for you to see her tomorrow."

"But I want to see her today! She's my mother!"

"Sorry." The static stopped and the intercom went dead.

Angry and disappointed, Sam backed away and started to turn around. A truck labeled *Kelly's Electronics and Repair* pulled up to the gate and stopped. Moments later, the gate opened and the truck eased through. Sam followed.

Nineteen

Dr. Kramer was studying the remains when Gordon arrived. He said he had just started, but he confirmed that they were of a female, that the epiphyses of the long bones had nearly closed which would be compatible with the age of menarche. She had been in the ground for ten to twelve years. He suggested Gordon go out for coffee and come back in an hour. Gordon stayed.

"Then have a cup here. Best coffee in town."

"No thanks, Doc. Gotta make a phone call. Is Harry around?"

"Just stepped out," volunteered the deputy. "Should be back soon."

The smell of the morgue turned Gordon's stomach and he turned away hoping to get a breath of fresh air. He was glad he never became a doctor, although it had been a great disappointment for his father. Law enforcement had become his choice of a career when he was a mere child of four. His uncle, a police officer, had given him a toy gun and a badge for Christmas. He wore them day and night—until he was six and the family dog carried the badge off and buried it. It was uncovered two years later when his mother planted a garden.

He hadn't thought about his parents much lately—nor his younger sister. The three had been killed in a head-on collision with a logging truck when he was in high school. His sister, an only sibling, was just ten—too young to die. After the funeral, he moved in with his uncle. That's when he made his final decision. He, too, would be a cop someday.

He poured himself a cup of coffee and sat down at Harry's desk. Harry Cantrell was his father's best man when he got married and his best friend right up until the day of the accident. Now he was the Medical Examiner for the State of Oregon. Gordon looked up at the picture on the wall: it had been there for as long as he could remember. It was of his father and Cantrell, each holding one end of a four-foot long salmon they had fished out of the mouth of the Columbia River.

He picked up the phone and punched in Sam's number. It rang several times before he hung up. Admitting defeat, he sat back and put his feet up on the desk.

"Take the couch. It's more comfortable," suggested the deputy.

Gordon didn't answer nor did he move. He was deep in thought. There was something about Fischer he didn't trust: the man was weasely, evasive. He didn't like his eyes and he didn't like the red hair: it looked artificial, dyed. Maybe it was a wig. And he didn't like his receptionist.

As he sifted through the evidence, sparse as it was, the case began to take on new perspective. Thinking back, he once again felt the guilt that had so often plagued him over the years: *the Ballard kidnapping should have been handled by someone else.*

The FBI had done their best, but with hundreds of abductions every year to investigate, not to mention other cases, they were dependent upon the cooperation and know-how of local authorities. Gordon was no expert back then; he was still wet behind the ears. O'Malley had placed too much confidence in him. But more important, he had broken a cardinal rule: he became emotionally involved, too close to the Ballard family—and Samantha.

He stood up and poured himself another cup of coffee: the smell of the lab was no longer noticeable. It was time to get to work, time to act like a police detective instead of a spoiled, sniveling kid.

He walked over to the table where Dr. Kramer was working. This time detached, he looked down at the body—or what was left of it—and said, "You know, Doctor, in 1991 out of 487 kidnap victims, 411 were eventually recovered."

Dumbfounded, the doctor stopped working. Without speaking, he looked up at the detective and waited.

"Seventy-six were never located."

Kramer continued to stare.

"Only thirteen percent of those recovered were found dead."

The anthropologist put down his instrument. "Lieutenant, what are you trying to tell me?"

"The seventy-six, Doctor. Maybe they weren't all kidnapped."

Samantha followed close behind Kelly's truck until it reached the front of the big house; then she turned and slowly drove to the back. She got out, quietly closed the car door and shuffled across dried leaves to the porch. As she was about to ascend the stairs, a window was slammed shut and a light went on inside. Fearing that she had been seen, she jumped back and attempted to blend into a bush.

This is ridiculous, she thought. *I'm not a detective. What am I doing here, playing hide-and-seek?*

Confident that she had not been seen, she eased up the stairs, crossed the porch and peered through the window. A short, fat woman in a dirty apron and a young, skinny girl wearing blue jeans were peeling potatoes. The woman kept jabbing the girl in the ribs with the handle of her knife as they peeled, the two laughing as they worked.

Sam ducked down, passed beyond the window and tried the back door. It squeaked as she inched it open; she waited to see if it had been noticed. No one came. Although warped, it opened easily. Sam slipped through and into the hall.

Through the kitchen door, she could hear the two giggling as she passed. A pleasant aroma of meat and spices wafted past her nose and she remembered she had not eaten since early morning. As she began to salivate, she hurried her pace through the hall until she found a stairway.

It had been several years since she visited her mother, but she remembered her room was on the second floor. *I hope they haven't moved her. If not, she will be on the south side of the building.*

Moving with caution, Samantha climbed the stairs, listening carefully for voices or signs of movement from above. As she approached the top of the stairs, she heard a man and a woman talking. They seemed to be moving her direction. Too late to descend the stairs and seek cover, she stooped low on the step. Shaking like a cornered wood mouse, she ducked her head into her lap and prayed she would not be seen.

"Increase the dosage to five-hundred milligrams, Nora. I'll sign the chart later," said the man.

"Yes, Doctor. And what shall I do about Mrs. Ballard?"

"Nothing. Nothing at all. I'll take care of her myself."

"Yes, Doctor. Do you want to see her now?"

"I'll talk to her. You can go. I won't be needing you anymore today."

The voices became softer as they continued on down the hall toward the front of the house. Samantha popped her head up and watched the man enter the last door on the right. Quickly she followed behind. The door was left ajar a few inches. Still shaking, she stood in the hall and listened.

"You're becoming a bit difficult, Mrs. Ballard. What seems to be the problem?"

The voice that followed was lethargic and halting. "I...I want to go...home."

"But you know you can't do that. You need your medication, you need therapy and you need me. We can't give you those things at home."

"I want to go...home," came the response.

"Well, we'll see. If you are very good, perhaps you can go home soon." A moment of silence followed before the doctor spoke again. "There, that will make you feel better."

Samantha peeked through the opening and saw the doctor recapping the needle on a syringe. She slipped across the hall and into an alcove seconds before the doctor opened the door and left.

Quickly, Sam ducked into her mother's room and closed the door behind her. She moved to the bed where her mother was fumbling with the covers and looked down at her.

"Mama?"

The sickly woman looked up and responded without hesitation. "Cindy, help me fix the covers. I'm cold."

Twenty

"You're in for a big disappointment, Wes." Juan Aguila took another bite from his sandwich. "You're trying to turn this case into something it isn't."

The two had met at the DugOut Deli a block from the precinct. Gordon wanted to bounce some of his ideas off the PI and they had been there in the semi-underground businessmen's hangout for over an hour discussing the case. Now, the detective was becoming uneasy. He still hadn't heard from Samantha. He had left three messages on her answering machine to call him on his pager, but it remained silent.

So did Gordon.

Aguila gulped down the last bite from his ham and cheese and took a sip from his Coke. "Face the facts, man. You've got a mother who crawled into a shell a month after her daughter was kidnapped—that's to be expected. You've got a devoted husband who..."

Gordon interrupted. "Wait a minute! I thought you didn't trust Ballard."

"I didn't say I didn't trust him. I said I think he has hormones, but he's taking good care of his wife and always has. Look at the house he bought her."

"A lot of good it's doing her now." Gordon leaned back in his chair and shook his head. "In my book, that doesn't buy it. There's more to life than money."

"Then you've still got him on your suspect list."

"Let's just say, I'm keeping all avenues open. Right now I'm concentrating on the redheaded shrink."

"And you want me to check him out. Okay, I'll get on it first thing in the morning. And the Hertz rental slip, and the phone calls to San Francisco, and...What else?"

"Everything you can find on Corelli. Everything! And I want to know when he bought the Hillsboro house."

Aguila was distracted by a buxom blonde hanging on the arm of a former client who was the owner of a large credit agency. Suspecting infidelity, he had recently retained Aguila to follow his wife. Aguila took the job, but she proved to be faithful. Now, here was the jerk—playing around.

"Juan, are you with me? She's not your type."

"Nope. Not at all," agreed the PI.

Preferring to avoid the man's eye, Aguila shifted his position just as Gordon's pager sounded. But it was too late: the amorous couple looked up and the man's face turned beet-red.

While Gordon went to the phone to answer the call, Aguila stood up, tossed a couple of bills on the table and picked up the ticket. The embarrassed man followed him to the cashier.

"Hey, it's not what you think. She's my sister."

"Yeah, sure, Mr. Davies. Your sister."

"Look, so she's not my sister. We met when I thought my wife was playing around. I came here to tell her it's over."

"You don't have to apologize to me, Mr. Davies. What you do is your business, not mine."

The man fumbled in his pocket, pulled out a twenty and surreptitiously tried to slip it into Aguila's hand. The PI jumped back.

"Hey, your tête-à-tête is safe: I never even saw you. And I don't want your money."

Mr. Davies stepped back and thanked him for his discretion. "If there's anything I can do for you, anything, just phone me."

"Sure, Mr. Davies, I will."

They decided to jog around the block before picking up the car to drive to the morgue. Harry had called and said they had completed the examination of the body.

"Who was the guy at the deli I saw you talking to?" Gordon asked between breaths.

"My ace in the hole," Aguila gasped. "He's going to be my source on Corelli."

"You're out of condition. What's his name?"

"Davies. He owns a credit agency and he's..." Aguila stopped to get a breath.

Gordon turned back, still jogging in place.

"You're right," said the PI. "I'm soft: it's my bum leg. He'll turn over anything you want to know on the shrink. He'll do it to keep my lip zipped."

The two started walking. "Find out about Rudy Fischer, too."

"You've got it!"

"Here it is, Wes. The full report." Harry handed the detective three computer pages of information.

"Give it to me straight, Harry. Do you think it's the Ballard girl?"

"Could be her. We'll know as soon as we get her dental records."

"When will that be?"

"Maybe tomorrow."

Without speaking, Samantha straightened the blankets and fluffed her mother's pillow while supporting her supple head. She held her hand as she relaxed into a deep sleep.

It's still Cindy. She was always her favorite: even now, she can't forget her.

Samantha never doubted that she was loved by her mother, but as a child, she knew she favored Cindy. Her father had balanced the attention, however, by devoting himself to Sam. He gave them both just about anything they wanted, but Sam received more praises for her accomplishments, of which there were many. Both the twins were talented and bright, but Sam was more industrious. Their father said it was because she was fifteen minutes older; the explanation always satisfied Cindy.

She looked down at the sleeping woman's face. The skin was aged and sallow and even in sleep she appeared troubled.

She couldn't bring herself to leave. She turned to look for a chair and saw the syringe the doctor had just used lying on the nightstand. It started the wheels turning in her head. She picked it up, stared at it for a moment and then slipped it in her handbag.

Realizing now that she had entered illegally and remembering that her car would eventually be noticed and investigated, Sam decided to leave. She kissed her mother on the forehead and left the room.

Moving swiftly through the hall and down the back stairs, she managed to reach the same door she had entered earlier without being seen. But there her luck ran out. As she reached for the doorknob, the kitchen door flew open and the fat woman in the dirty apron stepped into the hall.

Sam didn't wait or attempt to explain her presence. She flew out the door, jumped into her car and took off. Not knowing what to expect when she reached the gate, she tried to think of an excuse for her presence, but nothing came.

Maybe the gate will open automatically. Please, God, let the gate open.

But God did not hear. The gate remained shut.

Not knowing what to do next, Sam just sat there, waiting and quivering, expecting shots to ring out any moment, or a siren to blare.

But there was no gunfire and no siren. Instead, a voice came through the intercom, this time free from static. "Sorry, Miss

Kendall, I didn't see you drive up. And I like your hat. Have a nice evening." The gate swung open.

Twenty-One

The city lights were beginning to flicker and the streets were showing signs of Sunday nightlife. Across the Willamette, a fishing boat belched as it eased along the east bank headed for home. Gordon wondered where home was for the men aboard and if this trip was for pleasure or if they were out fishing on Sunday, too.

He liked to saunter through Tom McCall Park when he was discouraged or worried. Tonight he was worried: Sam had not called. He had tried her number six times since morning, and he was beginning to think she had freaked out after hearing the news of the body.

He was ready to head back to his apartment when he was distracted by a ruckus further down the park. Two white guys were beating up on a black; the black lay there taking it. He was tempted to walk to the nearest phone booth and report it, unidentified, but repented and started toward the commotion. He wasn't on duty, but he always carried his Glock under his coat and his Smith and Wesson at his ankle. He took the Glock from its holster and checked it out while he headed their way.

Before reaching the scene, a patrol car pulled up and he decided to let the officers handle it, but he stood at a distance and watched. They managed quite adequately without him. But he waited and watched anyway.

He hated it this way: racial beatings, shootings—and sometimes killings. His uncle had brought him up to think of all people as equal. They weren't. But he had to deal with them. That was his job.

The patrol car was taking them away now. He slipped the Glock back into its holster, then took it out again, sat on a bench and stared down at its smooth form. He was grateful for the security it had given him, but sorry he needed it. He recalled the day he got it from Fiscal Services: he thought it was a toy because it was so weightless. But a 9mm semi-automatic is no toy, even if it is partially composed of polymer plastic. It had served him well and saved his life more than once.

As he started back up the street, his pager sounded. He grabbed it to see who was calling: it was Samantha's phone number.

Gordon grabbed at his cell phone and dialed. She answered on the first ring.

"Wes, is that you? I've got to talk to you. I've been to see Mother. Can you drive out here?"

"I'm on my way."

Samantha was waiting at the door when he arrived. She pulled him in, pushed him onto the sofa, slammed the door shut and spoke before he had a chance to find out if she had heard the news.

"I know you're going to scold me for going back to the house, but I had to clean it before Dad came home." Without waiting for his response, she pulled up an ottoman, sat in front of him and said, "While I was there, I had another premonition...No, it was more than just a premonition or a *feeling*. It was some kind of...psychic connection. Wes, I could hear her voice calling out to me." She paused a moment, to see if he was focused on the importance of her message. He said nothing, so she went on. "This time she said, 'Hurry, Samantha, before it's too late! I need you!' It was *her voice*! She's in danger, Wes. I just know it!"

"How do you know it was *her* voice? You haven't heard it for years. Maybe you were hearing *your own* voice, Sam. Maybe it's just what you *wanted* to hear—to keep your hopes up." Wes could not detect whether she had heard the news, but he knew he had to prepare her for the inevitable.

Dejected, she stood and turned away from him.

He could feel her pain; he was sorry he had said what he said. To change the subject, he asked, "You went to see your mother?"

Sam felt abandoned by the only person she had ever fully trusted. She expected him to scoff at this, too—her reason for going to *Serenity*—but she said, "Yes, I had a feeling that *she* needed me, too."

Gordon leaned forward and stared at the floor. Before today, he was beginning to believe in her and her feelings, her premonitions—especially after seeing the girl with the box—but now they had found Cindy's body. Nevertheless, her murderer still had to be found and brought to justice.

"How was she? Did you talk to her?"

Her spirits renewed, Sam began her story. She told him about the visit to *Serenity*, the encounter at the gate, how she slipped in unseen, the conversation between the doctor and nurse, and the injection he had given her mother. She recounted everything down to the last detail and then reached into her pocket and took out the syringe. "I stole this, Wes. I want to know what he gave my mother."

Gordon berated her for entering *Serenity* without permission, but he couldn't help but admire her bravery and determination—and her cleverness for taking the syringe. He reached out and gingerly took it between two fingers. He studied it briefly and asked for a plastic bag.

While she was in the kitchen, he gave a sigh of relief. He felt certain she had not heard about Cindy's body.

Wes knew he would have to break the news to her before he left her apartment, but he continued to put it off. They spent most of the evening discussing the case; then, for the sake of conversation, he decided to tell her about Melanie Taylor. It didn't upset her that her father had a girlfriend and that she had a key to the house, but she couldn't accept the premise that they might be connected to the kidnapping.

"How can you think such a thing?" she shouted as she paced the floor. "Dad has always been devoted to us; he has always been hardworking and kind. Why would he do something so stupid? What would he have to gain?"

"Sam, I understand how you feel, but I have to keep an open mind."

Sam sat on the couch, thinking. Suddenly, she blurted, "Wes, I've been giving it a lot of thought lately. I think you're right about Maria. I think somehow she could have been involved."

He turned abruptly. "How's that?"

"I don't know. Maybe it's because I'm beginning to remember little things."

"What sort of little things?" This was what he wanted to hear. He needed to know as much about Sam's early family life as possible. He wanted to find Cindy's murderer, and he was beginning to question the motive for Carla Ballard's hospitalization. He remained silent while she collected her thoughts.

"Well, one thing I recall, when Cindy and I were about five or six, we took a trip—without Dad. They had argued. Mama waited for him to leave for work, then told us we didn't have to go to school." Sam paused, remembering. "She had Maria pack our bags and we all went to the beach for a couple of days. While we were there, Mama cried a lot and Maria consoled her. They talked a lot, too, but she tried not to let Cindy or me hear anything they said."

"Did you hear anything?"

"If we did, I don't remember what it was."

Gordon's first thought was *infidelity*, but Sam had already considered it.

"Wes, do you think Mama found out he was being unfaithful to her?"

Wes didn't respond; he was deep in thought.

She continued with her theory. "But even if he was unfaithful, even back then, that couldn't have had anything to do with Cindy's kidnapping."

"No, probably didn't. Who knows what they fought about; it could have been what color to paint the kitchen." Nevertheless, Wes made a mental note of the incident. "What else can you remember?"

"I remember getting up one night to go to the bathroom. I saw the light under the door of Dad's den. I went to the door and opened it. He turned and saw me."

"Yeah, go on."

"He was angry. He put a book...No, it was papers, or something. He put them in the desk drawer and locked it. He was upset that I caught him working in the middle of the night."

"Did he scold you?"

"He started to, then he calmed down, pulled me up on his knee and stroked and kissed me. He said I should never tell Mama that he was working at night like that, that it would worry her. He said it was to be our secret. He was always concerned about worrying Mama."

"Did you ever tell her?"

"No, he told me not to, but I told Maria. I told her the next day. Later, I caught her trying to pry open his desk drawer with a knife."

Somehow, Wes had gotten the impression that Samantha and Maria were not close. He was surprised that Sam had not kept the desk incident from Maria, too. Curious, he asked, "How come you told Maria?"

"I don't know. Guess I trusted her."

Wes sensed it was something else—something he had never been aware of before now. He decided to probe deeper. "Did you tell Cindy?"

"No! Maria told me *never* to tell Cindy!"

"Why, not? It doesn't seem that important to me."

Samantha's eyes became distant. She didn't respond.

"Sam?"

"You're right. I never thought of it that way. Cindy and I always told each other everything. I don't know why I kept it from her. Maybe it's because Maria was so adamant. She made me promise."

"How old were you then?"

"I don't remember: we were very small. Four, maybe five. Maria hadn't been with us very long."

Wes stood and wandered across the room. With hands pushed deep inside his hip pockets, he remained facing the wall with his back to her.

While she was waiting for him to continue the conversation, she remembered the letter. *He couldn't have found it; he would have mentioned it to me by now.*

Finally, he turned and faced her. "Sam, there's something you have to know." He looked down at his feet, shuffled them, then blurted out, "A body was found this morning—up in the woods near your home. They think it's Cindy." He wasn't prepared for her reaction.

"Yes, I know," she said calmly. "I heard it on the radio this morning. It isn't Cindy."

Twenty-Two

Gordon was ready to throw in the towel. Never had he been so provoked by her. Without regard for her feelings, he blew. "Sam, you are the most aggravating, stubborn, opinionated, bullheaded person I have ever known! Can't you hear what I've been telling you all these years? Cindy is dead! This morning they dug up her body. She's dead, girl. Why can't you accept that?"

Ignoring the outrage, Samantha stared out the window at the trees across the street for a moment and then turned slowly. Wes was standing there waiting, breathing heavily, feet firmly planted on the carpet and fists on his hips. He looked like a toreador waiting for the bull to charge. She snickered, controlled her amusement and snickered again. Unable to retain herself, she burst out laughing.

Gordon didn't think it was funny. It was her dead sister they were talking about. He threw his hands up in the air, spun around and fell into the recliner beneath him. *She's impossible!* he thought. *She's downright impossible!*

Sam's jocular mood changed. She looked at the distraught figure sprawled in the chair and felt his frustration. Before she realized what she was doing, she fell into his lap, put her arms around his neck and kissed him firmly.

He was shocked! She had never kissed him on the mouth before. Without thinking, he responded just as any hungry, virile man would do with a beautiful woman on his lap. He put his arms around her, held her tight and returned the kiss. It was a long and passionate kiss. It was what he wanted to do the day he saw her standing there in the champagne dress—the first day after she returned home—but he restrained himself then. And up until now.

Reluctantly, Sam pulled away. She felt warm and safe in his arms. She had fallen in love with him as a child, the love growing over the years from a childish infatuation to the way she felt now. She had tried to forget him when she was away—especially after receiving the letter—but when she returned, she knew it would be impossible. The love was still there, but it was no longer infatuation and she knew now that she could never give him the letter.

He was the first to speak. "Samantha, I didn't mean to do that." He gently dumped her off his lap and stood up, then took her hand and pulled her up from the floor. "I..."

Samantha put two fingers to his lips to hush him. She kissed him again gently and said, "Yes, you did. And so did I."

Wes wanted to scoop her up into his arms and take her to the bedroom, but he knew this wasn't the time—he knew he would regret it if he did. He hadn't yet sorted out his feelings—he had always thought of her as a child. *I'm too old for her; she's just a kid.* But he knew she was no longer "just a kid," and he was no longer convinced that thirteen years made that much difference—now.

Samantha felt his passion and pulled away. *Someday*, she thought, *but not now.*

She broke the spell by swatting him on the side of the head with a sofa pillow. "You still don't understand, do you? It's not Cindy!" she shouted. "The body they dug up is someone else. We've got to find her, Wes. She's out there somewhere calling for help!"

He was grateful for the distraction and followed through as if nothing had happened, but he knew now that there was no point in trying to convince her the body was Cindy. Maybe it wasn't: Harry's report was not yet conclusive. They would know tomorrow.

"You might be right, Sam," he said. "The body, I mean. Harry doesn't have her dental X-rays yet. The X-rays will tell us."

"They'll be wasting their..." Sam paused. "Wes, wait. There are no dental X-rays."

"What do you mean? You never went to a dentist?"

"Of course we went to a dentist, but he died a few years ago and his idiot wife threw them out. I tried to locate mine when I was at college and found out they were no longer available."

Twenty-Three

It was a beautiful Monday morning and it was going to be a good day for Detective Wesley Gordon: he could feel it in his bones. He sprinted down the stairs and out the front door, climbed into his car and lowered the top. The morning sun was warm. A purple finch flew from a nearby tree and landed on the hood of his car. It tilted its tiny head to the right and to the left and seemed to be asking for breakfast.

"Sorry, bird," he said. "Didn't bring anything with me. Stick around and tonight I'll order pizza for the two of us." The bird took flight and Gordon started the engine.

He began to whistle a tune—one from the seventies—but stopped when he realized he hadn't whistled in years. *Why now?* he thought. *What have I got to be happy about? Sam's brought nothing but trouble...*

Then his thoughts returned to the episode in the recliner last night. And he smiled.

O'Malley was hunched over the water fountain when he entered the precinct. The chief looked up, wiped the water from his mouth with his sleeve and waited. Gordon slowed his pace, then picked it up again as he approached him.

"Hold it right there, buddy. Okay, give me what you've got."

"Not much, Chief...Yeah, I've got something, but I need another day."

O'Malley took him by the elbow, steered him into his office, slammed the door and shoved him into a chair. He took his own chair and said, "Already gave you another day. Now tell me what you've got?"

"Nothing concrete, Boss, but I got held up by the weekend. I need to get into the bank."

The chief reached into his pocket for a wallet. "I'll loan you a buck. Now, give me the scoop."

Gordon briefed the chief on his weekend activities and included his encounter with Fischer. Without limiting words, he expressed his distrust of the guy.

"Okay, Gordon, you just bought another twenty-four hours, but that's it: we've got to let the Feds in. We've run a tracer on all kids that disappeared from the area back then and the Ballard kid's as good a possibility as any, I'm sorry to say. We'll know soon. The dental records will confirm it."

"No they won't." Gordon repeated Samantha's story about the dentist's wife for the second time—he'd told Harry earlier when he dropped off the syringe.

"Now we'll never know," barked the chief.

Gordon grinned. "Unless we go DNA on the remains," he added, widening his grin sagaciously.

"What are you going to use for a match?"

"We've got an identical twin."

O'Malley sat upright. "Then get on it, Gordon. What are you waiting for, Christmas?"

Harry was eagerly awaiting his arrival when the detective entered. The lab had run the test on the syringe and the residue proved to be diazepam, propylene glycol, ethyl alcohol and buffers, better known as Valium, a strong sedative not generally given to depressed patients. Analysis showed that the plunger had been pulled back two centimeters and that 2 cc's of Valium had been injected. Ten milligrams is far too much for an already sedated patient. Ordinarily, this dosage is given to someone having a prolonged seizure such as status epilepticus. Continued use of even five milligrams would lead to further depression, not only emotionally, but of the respiratory system as well. It could cause the patient to stop breathing, or bring on cardiac arrest, especially in a debilitated patient. Harry suggested that Mrs. Ballard's hospital records be subpoenaed to see if periodic blood counts and liver function tests were being done. Gordon made a mental note to get the subpoena, and then he suggested the DNA match for the remains of the body they had found.

"Yeah, sure, we could give it a whirl. They'll need Sam's blood."

"They've got it!" confirmed Gordon.

The telephone operator at the studio put him right through. Sam agreed to go to the lab as soon as she got off work. She wasn't happy about having her blood drawn, but she was willing to do anything to prove the body was not Cindy's. "I'll do it if you buy me dinner after," she said. "Pick me up at six."

The next stop was the bank. He had no problem getting a photocopy of Corelli's signature for Aguila—it would be needed for comparison of the signature at the Hertz car rental—but Corelli's bank records turned out to be a disappointment. They showed that the twenty-five hundred dollar monthly deposits were all cash which told him nothing, except that there may have been a reason for covering up its source. Illegal? Laundered? Maybe. But there wasn't time to look into it now. He was to meet Aguila at the deli in ten minutes.

The PI ordered his usual ham and cheese; Gordon ordered *just coffee.* "No, make that milk," he said, changing his mind. His stomach was acting up again.

"Gordon, you've gotta quit the force," Aguila said. "You're going to end up in the hospital again."

"Yeah, I know, and become a PI, like you. Is your life any easier?"

"At least I'm my own boss."

"I like a steady salary."

The two bantered back and forth, then got down to business. Gordon pulled out the paper that had Corelli's signature and handed it over to the PI.

"No good," he said. "I've already checked: Hertz records don't go back that far. But I dug up something from personnel you'll like. Remember Vic Porter, the clerk that handled the paperwork on the rental car?"

"Yeah, what about him?"

Aguila put a hold on his answer. The waitress was standing there with their order, waiting for them to clear a spot on the table.

"He quit right after he got out of the hospital."

Gordon didn't follow. He gave Aguila a blank stare and waited for the PI to swallow his first bite.

"The broad that gave me the dope said he'd been with the company for six years, loved his job and made good money. But he just up and quit for no reason. Didn't even give notice."

"How come she remembered so well? Been a long time."

"She had the hots for him."

"Did they shack up?"

"Nope, she was hired just a month before he quit. Said it never got that far."

"Was she there when Jones signed up for the car?"

"Yup, and Jones was a redhead."

Twenty-Four

The phone call from Wes made it difficult for Sam to concentrate. She had been given the assignment to gather statistics on the influx into the greater Portland area and its effects on traffic and she was now feverishly organizing them on her computer. The station had decided to do a special that was to follow the evening news and they were ready to give Sam a piece of it—on camera. It excited her, even to the point of diverting her attention from Cindy, but Wes's phone call interfered. Population and traffic problems were now furthest from her mind.

Having taken a course in genetics at college, she was well aware of DNA and its role in heredity. *Deoxyribonucleic acid.* Silently, she repeated the words over and over, trying to remember all she had learned about its use in forensic medicine. She was about to log off her word processor and into an encyclopedia for information retrieval when she remembered the station had an extensive library.

Sam headed for the small room on the fourth floor, switched on the light and pulled two books on forensic medicine from the shelf. The first book was outdated and gave no information on DNA matching. The second book was not recent, but a full chapter was devoted to the subject. Sam settled down and started reading.

Although decomposition of the body may, in time, leave little more than hair, nails, bone and fragments of tissue, genetic fingerprinting (DNA matching) is now being widely used internationally to pinpoint identity. The genetic code of every individual is different, no two persons having the same genetic heritage— with one exception, that of identical twins or other identical multiples.

Sam's head was swimming. What if her blood sample proved the remains at the morgue are those of her twin sister? She had no difficulty remembering her college course and that the fingerprints of identical twins are dissimilar, but having developed from a single zygote, their DNA is the same.

Sam closed the book, sat on the stepstool at her feet and began to think. Once again, she reasoned that years of hope and desire could be responsible for her premonitions and that she had not truly accepted adulthood. Wes was right: she was still just a child. It was time for her to accept the possibility that Cindy was gone, that bits and pieces of her body were lying on a cold slab at this very moment and that someone had murdered her.

As she was sitting there, shoulders hunched and hands wringing, the letter came to mind. Now, she realized she had to turn it over to Wes. But the letter was gone—perhaps never to be found. It might have been the only piece of evidence that would lead to Cindy's murderer.

Trying desperately to recall the content of the letter, she remembered the typing and how sloppily the letters were formed—obviously the fault of an old and dirty typewriter. The dream she had the night before came into view and she knew why the O's were attacking her. In the letter, they had been slightly raised. The scene disturbed her—she didn't know why—and something in her past was nibbling away at her subconscious.

"What is it?" she said aloud. "Why did I have that stupid dream? Why the O's!"

Someone who had just entered the library called out to her. "Hello, you talking to me?"

Sam stood. "Oh, no, no. I was just thinking about...It's nothing." She forced a smile, replaced the book on the shelf and left without introducing herself.

Walking back to her desk, she remembered what it was about the letter that disturbed her: it had been typed on an old Underwood that had belonged to her grandmother—and later to her father.

Twenty-Five

It was one thirty-five when the two left the deli. Juan Aguila sniffed the air and climbed into his car to return to his office. He would call Davies and pressure him for the information on Fischer and Corelli, he told Gordon as he waved good-bye. "Want a ride to the court house?" he yelled out the window. "Smells like rain coming."

"No thanks, I'll walk," Gordon answered. He needed the exercise, and he could think better when he was alone.

Gordon headed up the street towards the courthouse to pick up a subpoena for Mrs. Ballard's medical records. Maybe he would ask for a search warrant as well. He wasn't sure what he expected to find, but he knew there was something fishy going on out there, and he was determined to find out what it was.

It had been years since he'd functioned with a full head of steam, and he was beginning to feel like a detective again. He often wondered why the chief hadn't thrown the book at him, especially after he'd botched the murder case that he and Aguila were on, the one that got his best friend and partner shot up. No one blamed him. They even tried to convince him it wasn't his fault, but if he hadn't ended up in the hospital with a bleeding ulcer, he'd have been there where he belonged, at Aguila's back, and Aguila wouldn't have taken a bullet. It should have been his, the bullet, right in his head. That was four years ago. Since then, O'Malley had thrown him cases that any rookie could solve. But he didn't care: emotionally, he wasn't up to much more.

Now, his ulcer was acting up again. But it was excitement this time that was making the gastric juices flow, not depression. Or disappointment.

Maybe that's why Gordon's interest in Mrs. Ballard was renewed. He'd been there, too. He knew what depression was and what it could do to a guy. It could destroy your reason for living. Coupled with guilt, it could eat away at your guts until you wanted to crawl into a dark hole and...

Gordon paused and looked up at the sky when a drop of rain landed on his cheek. *Should have taken my car*, he thought, picking up his pace.

He didn't want to think about those days, the days when nothing went right, when he had been forced to see a shrink or lose his job. Why do they always think you're going to blow your brains out when something goes wrong? If you're not strong enough to handle it, you have no business being on the force. Maybe that's it: can you handle the pressure and make mistakes without thinking the world has come to an end? He got through it, but he could have done it without the shrink.

He stopped and bought a Gelato.

Gordon's thoughts turned to Carla Ballard again. He was convinced she'd be better off without Dr. Fischer, especially after hearing about the shot he'd given her. Valium? No way. He'd refused it when he was in the hospital—he didn't want to get hooked—but he didn't know how serious the side effects could be until Harry told him this morning.

Gordon licked his lips, tossed the remainder of the ice cream cone in a waste can and started jogging. He was anxious to see Carla Ballard again. But this time, the ball would be in his field—he would call the shots.

Highway 26 was jammed with traffic. It wasn't normal for mid-afternoon on a Monday, but there was construction again. *Maybe tomorrow*, he thought, as the traffic came to a halt.

No, he had the subpoena and the warrant in his pocket and tomorrow was too far off. If he didn't make it back in time to pick up Sam at six, he'd call her to go on home. They could draw her blood tomorrow.

He was tempted to use his emergency lights, but it was against regulations in a non-emergency. *Walker would have done it,* he thought. But then, television can get away with anything. By the time he pulled up to the gate at *Serenity*, it was a quarter to four.

Doctor Fischer wasn't available when he arrived, but he had no problem getting in: the husky-voiced receptionist knew what a warrant was and she called a nurse to escort him to Mrs. Ballard's room. The medical records would be brought to him later, she said.

Carla Ballard was sitting in a chair near an open window. Decorative wrought-iron bars attached to the outer framework prevented one from falling out. Or jumping. Her eyes were fixed on something outside. The nurse walked over to her and with a gentle voice called her by name before she touched her on the shoulder. "Mrs. Ballard, you have a visitor."

The patient, still fascinated by something in the trees, ignored her. The nurse spoke again.

"They're still there, Cindy. See them? High up in the trees." Mrs. Ballard raised her arm from the chair and pointed.

"She's hallucinating again," explained the nurse.

"Does she do that often?" asked Gordon.

"Oh, yes, all the time. It only lasts for a moment. If you ask her what's in the trees, she'll come out of it and won't even remember what she saw."

"Why did she call you *Cindy*?"

"She calls everyone Cindy."

"Has she always done that?"

"Uh, huh. For as long as I've been here."

"And how long has that been?" asked the detective.

"Two-and-a-half years."

"How many employees does the doctor have?"

"Not many," she said. "He likes doing things himself—especially when there are so few patients. Right now, we only have four. Wants to save money, I think. He's kind of a skinflint. Doesn't pay much either."

"Is that uncommon? Not having many patients, I mean."

"Not lately," she said, with a snort and a shrug of her shoulders.

Gordon edged closer to the woman in the chair. "Is it okay if I talk to her?"

"Of course, but she'll think you're a doctor."

Gordon walked to the window and looked out. He stooped down to level his shoulders with hers and said, "Yes, I can see them, Mrs. Ballard. What are they doing?"

Much to his surprise, the woman answered. "They're nibbling at the branches, Doctor. Someday they'll nibble all the way through and there won't be anymore branches. You really should do something about it. The trees are so beautiful and they have a soul, too, just like we do. It must be very painful for them."

Gordon squinted and looked more closely at the trees, then turned and looked into the woman's eyes. Mrs. Ballard returned the gaze. "You're not a doctor," she said. "Who are you?"

"I'm a detective, Carla. My name is Wesley Gordon. Do you remember me?"

Mrs. Ballard furrowed her brow, tilted her head and stared for a moment, then reached out and touched him on the cheek. "Yes,…I remember you," she said, hesitantly. "You're the nice man that fixed my window. I didn't mean to break it. It was an accident, you know."

Gordon continued to role-play. "Of course, you didn't. We know that." He wanted to be alone with her, to ask questions without the nurse there, but he knew she wouldn't leave his side. He was about to try, at least, by asking her to fetch Mrs.

Ballard's chart, when a woman walked in with it. She handed it to the detective.

Not wanting to break the rapport he had established with Mrs. Ballard, he laid the chart on the floor. Again he looked into the distant eyes of the woman he had once known so well and realized she had become someone else. Now, her face was wan, her body was frail and her mind was gone. But forever? Would she always be like this? He looked out at the trees and wondered. *Perhaps not. Maybe it's not too late*, he thought. If only he could break through the veil that clouded her memory...

His thoughts were interrupted by a voice at the door. "Well, Detective, it appears we have the pleasure of your visit again. And so soon?" Doctor Fischer waved the nurse out and walked in. "I hope you're not disturbing Mrs. Ballard. She's very sensitive, you know."

Gordon picked up the chart and stood. He stretched out his hand, but the doctor refused to shake it. "I'm aware of the fragility of these people, Doctor, and I'm sure I have not disturbed her. Could we go somewhere and talk?"

Carla Ballard reached out for him. "No, don't go. I like him, Doctor. Don't take him away."

The doctor steered the detective toward the door speaking as they left. "He can come back again sometime, Mrs. Ballard. You need to rest now."

The two men walked down the hall to the stairway. As they began to descend, the nurse started up. When she passed by, she brushed the detective with her arm. Furtively and without looked at him, she slipped something into his pocket. Gordon said nothing. He followed the doctor down the stairs and into his office. He would check his pocket later.

Twenty-Six

The French doors to the veranda were standing open and the doctor ambled through. Gordon followed. Pots of geraniums, azaleas and nasturtiums were strategically located between larger containers of conifers that had been carefully pruned into peculiar shapes. Two gigantic rhododendrons planted too close to the building had reached the veranda and were intruding upon their space. The doctor moved to the railing and delicately plucked off a few dead leaves, placing them in his pocket. Then, with arms folded across his chest and leaning against the railing, he looked at the detective head on.

"A warrant wasn't necessary, Lieutenant. We would have been more than happy to have you visit our patient had you made an appointment first."

Gordon walked to the railing and leaned over to inspect the property below. Latticework covered with ivy hugged the wall. It would be a twelve-foot drop to the ground—if one found it necessary to leave in that manner. He looked out at the expansive grounds and took a mental photo of the buildings, trees and pathways. An old carriage house, tilting precariously, was sheltered between large pines two hundred feet away. Just beyond and snuggled under tall spruce was the guesthouse Fischer had once lived in. It looked neglected now. To the right, by craning his neck, he could see part of the main gate. Apparently, someone had just entered as it was in the process of closing.

Gordon moved to a small, white ornamental table, placed the chart on it and sat on a matching chair. He opened the chart and began thumbing through the pages. It was not filled with copious notes as he expected, but they began ten years prior, each notation carefully dated. He noticed several different styles of handwriting, many of which were of the various nurses recording their observations of the patient. Doctor Fischer's handwriting was neat and small, but not easily deciphered. Another handwriting, frequent during the first few years but later seldom found, was even more illegible, scrawling and copious. Whoever wrote the notes had much to say, but apparently didn't want anyone to know what it was. Gordon couldn't read the signature.

He looked for lab reports and found none. *Only notes?* he thought. *Seems odd. Surely there were blood tests, EKG's and electroencephalograms done.*

"I don't see any lab work, Doctor."

"We don't do lab work here. It's not necessary."

Gordon was tempted to question the doctor's reasoning, but decided to hold the argument for later. He wanted to retain his good nature—for now.

Holding out the subpoena, he said, "I would like to borrow the chart for a few days if I may, or if you prefer, a copy will do. Do you have a machine?"

"We'll make you a copy. But why are you interested, Lieutenant? Mrs. Ballard is getting excellent care. Is someone suing us?"

"The subpoena would come from an attorney if that were so. No, you're not being sued. It has to do with the kidnapping of Cindy Ballard; we have reopened the case."

The doctor shifted his position and began grooming another plant. His eyes darted about, avoiding those of the detective. "You have new clues?"

"Apparently you don't watch television, or you would know. The remains of a body have been dug up that may prove to be the Ballard twin."

"So that makes it murder."

"That's correct."

The doctor resumed the grooming of his plants, his interest in the discovery seemingly minimal. "You don't plan to tell Mrs. Ballard, I hope. I don't want you to tell her."

"Would she understand?"

"Not really. She doesn't remember her daughter at all."

"But she calls the nurses *Cindy*."

"It means nothing. It's just a name she frequently uses for want of another: she can't remember their names."

Gordon got to his feet, produced the warrant and handed it to the doctor. "I'd like to look around, Doctor. Do you mind?"

"It seems I have no choice." The doctor walked through the veranda door and back into his office. "Do as you please: we have nothing to hide." He left the room.

Gordon took the chart to the receptionist. Leaving the subpoena on her desk, he asked that a copy be prepared and told her he'd pick it up later.

The tour of the building shed no light on possible illegal activities, but he wondered how long it had been since the hospital had been inspected by the health department. The housekeeper must be on booze, he thought. Recalling the conversation he'd just had with the nurse, he decided Fischer did the cleaning himself—to save money. Yet, Fischer's office was spotless and he seemed immaculate in his own personal appearance.

An Asian, built like a bulldog and probably capable of tearing the Portland phone book in half with little effort, had followed him around like a puppy dog. He never spoke once during the hour he was with the detective, and Gordon wondered if he was mute. Disappointed, Gordon returned to the receptionist's desk and the guide disappeared. The receptionist had the copies ready.

By the time he reached the highway, he calculated he would just have time to make it to the television studio by six if the traffic cooperated. Then he remembered the nurse had slipped something into his pocket. He pulled over and removed three sheets of neatly folded paper. They were reports—lab reports on Carla Ballard.

Gordon dropped the reports off for Harry to interpret. "I'll call you later. Gotta pick up Sam," he said, rushing out.

She was in the champagne dress again, standing there just as she had done five nights before when he saw her for the first time in five years. So much had happened in those few days it seemed she had been back for months.

She climbed in, closed the door and gave him a peck on the cheek. The blood in his veins surged hot, and he found himself wanting to take her to his apartment rather than to the police lab. He shook the thought from his head and pulled away from the curb.

"Have a good day?" she asked.

"Real good," he answered, not really wanting to talk about it.

They had reached the freeway before another word was spoken. Sam sensed he was deep in thought and remained silent. Finally, she could hold her curiosity no longer.

"Where have you been? Have you found out anything about Cindy?"

He was not quick to answer, and she asked again.

"No, there's nothing new on her, but I'm convinced there's a connection..." He paused for a moment and then blurted, "Sam, we've got to get your mother out of that hospital."

The remark was unexpected, but welcome. "Wes, I came to that conclusion yesterday. But how?"

"Is your father back from Reno yet?"

"Yes, he flew in late last night. He called me this morning from the bank."

"I think it's time we had a long talk with him."

While the tech was drawing Sam's blood, Wes called Aguila.

"Nothing yet, Gordon," the PI said. "But Davies promised to have something for me by tomorrow morning. I told him to dig up everything he could from every source available. He said he would, that he owed it to me."

"He was covering his fanny."

"He should have covered it a lot sooner," Aguila added. "Learn anything at the hospital?"

"Enough to convince O'Malley there's more to this case than we thought."

"Then they're sure?

"About what?"

"That it's Cindy: the remains they dug up."

"No, not yet, but I am."

"Have you told Sam?"

"Can't do that. Not till the DNA proves it, and that'll take at least a couple of weeks. Longer, if the PCR isn't conclusive.

"How long does that take—whatever that is?" asked the PI.

"Have no idea, but it's a complicated process that I don't understand. Ask Janet someday: she'll tell you."

"Who's Janet?"

"She's the gal that does the DNA's. Sharp cookie, too. I'll introduce you sometime: she's single. Gotta call Harry. Let me know the minute you have something."

"Right."

Harry went over Mrs. Ballard's lab reports with Gordon, pointing out the inconsistencies. A blood chemistry panel done shortly after she was admitted was essentially normal. Another was done a year later: it showed she was anemic and hypothyroid. A third, done three months ago, indicated some liver damage along with continuation of the anemia and hypothyroidism. The test that concerned him the most, however, was the elevated serum osmolality. "That's not good, Gordon."

"Why? What does it mean?"

"Diabetes, maybe, in which case it wouldn't have been ordered unless she was very, very sick. Who's this gal's doctor?" he said as he squinted, scrutinizing the signature that ordered the lab test. "Hmm, Anthony Corelli. Never heard of him."

Twenty-Seven

The name *Corelli* hit Gordon like a midwest cyclone. He confirmed it with Harry, thanked him for the information and slammed the phone into its cradle.

Samantha was still tugging at her pantyhose when Gordon burst into the women's restroom. Snatching her by the arm, he fled out the door and down the hall. "Hey, hold on a minute!" she howled, pulling her skirt down with her free hand. "Have you gone crazy?"

"I was never more sane," he responded, dragging her along as he barged through the elevator door.

Outside, traffic was wild. It had started to rain and pedestrians were darting about hoping to get to their cars before getting wet. Gordon shoved Sam into the passenger seat of his car and rushed around to the driver's side, almost knocking a woman to her feet. He apologized, jumped into the car and turned the key in the ignition. As he pulled away from the curb, Sam stared at him waiting for an explanation. They were halfway to the Ballard home before he told her about the lab reports and that Corelli had ordered tests.

Stunned by the news, Samantha responded in disbelief. "But, Wes, why would Maria's husband be ordering lab..." She paused and then continued as if by revelation. "Of course. Maria found out about mother's illness and talked her husband into seeing her."

"Sam, you're so naive."

Samantha was disturbed by Wes's comment—he was still treating her like a child—but rather than to start another argument, she suppressed her indignation.

"I'm saying your mother's in danger and Corelli's responsible. We've got to get her out of there. We need your dad to sign the release."

She hesitated. She still hadn't told Wes about the letter, but she couldn't convince herself that her father had typed it. Yet, she knew it was his typewriter. Why would he say those things about Wes, and why would he want to harm him, of all people? They had always admired and respected each other.

"Wes, stop the car."

He glanced at her, but continued to drive.

"Wes, we can't go to Dad now. Stop the car!" Reluctantly, she added, "He may be involved."

Gordon pulled over and faced her. With his left arm draped across the steering wheel and right arm across the back of the seat, he waited—patiently. The rain was pounding the car so loudly now he thought he might not have heard correctly. He didn't *want* to hear her say it; he had convinced himself that Mr. Ballard was innocent of all but infidelity, but he wasn't surprised. Too many things were pointing that direction.

"Wes," she finally said with eyes diverted, "did you find a letter in your car? A small envelope with my name typed on the front?"

"No, no envelope."

She reached down and felt under the seat. There was only the wrench that he always kept there—a backup weapon. Now she knew where the letter was: she had left her handbag on the upstairs hall commode while she was looking for photos of Maria. Her father must have gone through it and removed it; it could be no other place. She felt empty. A feeling of dizziness came over her when she realized he might be responsible for all the years of heartbreak and agony her mother had gone through.

Wes was still waiting for an explanation. Finally, Sam told him about the lost letter and that she had received it a few days before leaving for Seattle.

"What did it say?" Facetiously and imitating the voice of a gossipy housewife, he added, "I'm dying of curiosity."

"It's not funny, Wes, it's serious! You won't like it when you hear it!"

"Sorry, Kitten, I didn't mean to mock you. It's just that you made it sound so ominous."

"Maybe it is. I wish I had it so I could read it word for word, but I remember it pretty well. This is what it said." She gulped and began. *"Your sister is dead! Accept it, or you will end up like your mother,..."* Sam paused, then continued, *"...and he will be dead!* He meant *you*, Wes. I couldn't risk your life. The letter threatened your life if I revealed its presence to anyone."

Wes was livid. "Woman, why didn't you tell me about this before? How could you be so stupid!"

"I thought it was the work of a prankster, but I still couldn't gamble on your life and I knew Cindy wasn't dead." Her voice dropped. "But now I think Dad wrote it."

Gordon straightened up, ran his hands over his face, and then gripped the steering wheel to control his outrage. With forced calmness he said, "What makes you think your dad wrote it?"

"When Cindy and I were children, he would let us play with an old typewriter that Grandma had given him. I remember the O's were slightly raised. In the letter, the O was raised the same way."

"And you kept this quiet all this time? Sam, I can't believe you would be so stupid! Where's the typewriter now?"

"I don't know; I haven't seen it in years." Hoping to defend herself, she said, "Wes, I never thought about the typewriter until today; I'd forgotten about it. And the letter seemed like a big joke! I was going to give it to you the night we went to

Charley's, but we got in an argument, then we were caught up in conversation about Maria. It slipped my mind."

"Sam, that letter could be the evidence we are looking for. It could lead us to Cindy's kidnapper."

"I'm sorry; I just didn't think it was important. I never thought of it as evidence."

"You should have let me decide that. It's what I do for a living, you know." He calmed himself and remained silent, thinking. Sam studied his expression, hoping to get a hint of what his next move would be. It was several moments before he turned to her and said, "Sam, I hate to have to tell you this, but I think your father has kept your mother in that hospital all these years in order to…"

She interrupted. "I know what you're going to say, and I know why Dad sent the letter. He didn't want me to return and spoil his affair with his girlfriend. He was taking advantage of Cindy's abduction to keep me away. Wes, how could he do such a thing?"

He was sorry now that he had insulted her intelligence. She was hurt, and although he didn't agree with her, he wanted to comfort her. "Don't get carried away. We don't know. You can't accuse him of something that's strictly theory: we need proof. He may be perfectly innocent." He didn't believe it, but now was not the time to tell Sam what he did suspect.

"But the letter!"

"It could have been typed by someone else." Wes had Melanie Taylor in mind. Or Maria. Maybe Mrs. Ballard had given the typewriter to Maria. Someone wanted Sam to remain in Seattle where she couldn't stir up trouble—or get the case reopened. Someone was desperate enough to try childish measures to keep her away. Now, more than ever, Wes Gordon was certain they were onto something.

Sam squirmed and shifted her position. "I hadn't thought of that," she said. "But you're right: the typewriter disappeared before Maria was fired. Maybe Mama gave it to her." She looked him directly in the eye. "You still think she's the kidnapper, don't you?"

"Like I said, I have to keep an open mind. But right now I'm concerned about your mother. We've got to get her out of that hospital before they pump anymore Valium into her—and God only knows what else." He started the engine and pulled away from the curb. "We'll have to chance it, and if your father won't sign a release, I'll get a writ on wrongful commitment. We'll take her to your apartment; I don't want her to go home."

A car was in the driveway when they arrived at the Ballard house. Gordon recognized it immediately: it was Melanie's. He pulled up in front, doused the headlights and turned off the engine. *This is going to screw things up*, he thought. Reluctantly, he said, "Are you ready to meet your father's girlfriend?" Not waiting for an answer, he opened his door, got out and walked around to help Sam from the car. She didn't need help: she was already out by the time he got there.

"Is she pretty?" she asked not really wanting to know.

"She wouldn't win a beauty contest, if that's what you mean."

At the front door Sam took out her keys and opened it slowly. "Dad?" she called out tentatively. There was no answer.

The living room was dim with only an accent light casting an eerie glow. There were no other lights on downstairs and no evidence of anyone in the house. Upstairs the hall light was on. Samantha started up.

"Wait," said Wes touching her arm. "Listen."

Then she heard it. There were tiny squeals of joy coming from above. Softly she said, "Wes, I don't think I can take this." She backed down and headed toward the front door.

He grabbed her arm and whispered, "You were bound to find out sooner or later. You might as well confront him now."

"Now?" she said with an astonished squeak.

"Now. But let's be discreet." He quietly opened the front door, led Sam out, and then closed it. He rang the bell.

It was several moments before the door opened. Mr. Ballard stood there, fully dressed in greasy clothes and with a screwdriver in his hand. "Wes, Sam, come in. Did you forget your keys? Sorry I took so long. I was in the garage fixing the car."

Twenty-Eight

Dumbfounded, the two turned and looked at each other, neither knowing what to say. Uttering inaudible clichés, Gordon brushed the rain from his coat, while Sam watched the droplets fall to the floor. She was about to make excuses for not using her keys when an attractive woman in her late thirties appeared at the top of the stairway. She was dressed in a white blouse and gray slacks. A scarf was wrapped around her head and she held a rag in her hand.

Ballard looked up. "Melanie, come meet my daughter," he said, extending his hand upward in a beckoning gesture.

The woman draped the rag over the railing, rubbed her hands on her clothes and descended the stairs. She reached out for Samantha's hand. "It's about time I got to meet you. Your father talks about you incessantly, and now I can see why."

Ballard introduced her to Gordon and they moved into the living room.

"Melanie cleans for me now and then. You two look cold and wet. Coffee?" Without waiting for an answer, he looked at Melanie and conveyed a message.

"I'll get it. And I think we could use a little heat," she said, touching the thermometer as she passed through the hall. Sam resented her obvious familiarity with the house and the manner in which she displayed control over the situation.

Gordon watched Ballard's expression as he positioned himself on the sofa. He tried to appear at ease, but he didn't waste time explaining.

"I probably should have told you about Melanie long ago, Sam, but I was afraid you wouldn't understand. She and I, you see, have been investing in property together so we spend a lot of time with each other. She's a real estate agent and comes across good deals now and then. We just purchased a plot of land in Reno that we hope to develop sometime in the future."

So that's what the five thousand dollars was for, thought Gordon. The revelation was almost disappointing: he had imagined it was for something more exotic.

Ballard went on, but his discomfort became obvious when he repeated his earlier statement. "Melanie has been good enough to clean house for me when it needs it." Avoiding Sam's eyes, he looked down at the floor and then glanced at Gordon. "I suppose I should have told you when you called me at Reno and asked if anyone else had a key, but I didn't want to explain then. It was Melanie that came in that day: I needed some papers off my desk. She brought them to Reno…"

Samantha interrupted. "Dad, it's okay. I understand."

"No, you don't understand." Her father was becoming tense. "After your mother went away, I…"

She interrupted again. "It's okay, Dad: you were lonely. There's no need to explain."

Gordon broke in. He wanted to get to the subject of Mrs. Ballard's release before Melanie returned, but it was too late. She entered with a tray in her hands. He would have to discuss the matter in front of her. "Jim, I've been out to visit Carla and I don't like what I see. I think she's being medicated too heavily. I don't trust her doctor…or rather, her doctors."

"Doctors? She only has one: Dr. Fischer."

"No," he corrected. "She has two." Gordon watched the man's face carefully. He seemed sincere and confused.

"No," Ballard said adamantly. "She has just one doctor. Doctor Fischer has been treating her the entire time."

Gordon accepted a cup of coffee from Melanie, took a sip and continued. "Then you don't know about Doctor Corelli?"

"Corelli? The name sounds familiar." Ballard didn't so much as raise an eyebrow. "Oh, yes, I believe he checked in on Fischer's patients occasionally—whenever he was away. A locum tenens, no doubt."

Although Ballard's clouded awareness of the man seemed genuine, Gordon studied him judiciously as he said, "No, he has been seeing her regularly—especially at the beginning." Gordon weighed his next comment carefully and then decided to gamble the information. "He's the man Maria Gonzales married. Perhaps you didn't know she married a..."

Ballard was livid. Unable to control his anger, he shouted, "Maria Gonzales? That bag of...! She has no right..." He realized his response and lack of control had shocked both Melanie and his daughter so he lowered his voice. "How did Corelli get involved? Who gave him permission to attend my wife?" He looked to each of them for an answer.

Samantha spoke up. "Dad, we don't know yet how Doctor Corelli became involved. We thought *you* might tell *us*."

Her father stood up and took several paces away from them, then turned and glared at Sam. "You know I would never allow him to treat your mother. I forbade her years ago to ever see that woman again! And I had no idea she had married a doctor!"

"Then you knew she got married?" followed Gordon.

"Yes, I knew she got married, but I never met the guy, nor did I know his name!" Ballard was shouting again.

Now Samantha became short-fused. She jumped to her feet and shouted back. "Why, Dad, why did you make Maria leave? Cindy and I loved her. And mother—she loved her, too. What did Maria ever do to you?"

"I never trusted her! She was a snoop. She..."

Ballard had said too much. He had never lost control before in front of his daughter, and he suddenly became aware of

Melanie's bewilderment. Wisely, she remained silent. He apologized.

Gordon picked up where he left off. "Like I was saying, Jim, I believe Carla's in danger. I think you should get her out of there. Sam's willing to take care of her, to take her to her apartment."

The irate man had calmed himself. He took his seat and spoke softly. "I want only the best for my wife. No, if you think she should be released, I'll bring her here. I'll hire a nurse to stay with her. I had no idea she was being abused: Doctor Fischer seemed very competent." His voice rose again. "And I had no idea he was allowing anyone else to treat her! You know that, Wes. You and I went out there together to check out the place."

"I know, Jim. I had Fischer run through the computer; we found nothing on him."

"It was what Carla wanted. She asked to be taken there after we…" Ballard sat up, rigid. "It was Maria! She knew!"

"Knew what?" Sam asked.

"She knew…" Ballard backed down. "Nothing, nothing."

Gordon didn't like the connotation. Something was there, something significant. He repeated Sam's question. "She knew what, Jim?"

"Like I said: nothing. It isn't important." He stood. "I think you're right: Carla should come home tonight."

"Then you'll go with us?"

"Yes. No, I'll give you a letter of release. You and Sam go pick her up immediately while I prepare her room and hire a nurse. She can stay in your room, Sam, where she'll be comfortable. The nurse can take the guest room. I'll call Fischer now and tell him you're coming." He suddenly remembered the woman who had remained so silent. "Melanie, would you help me with the sheets, please, then I think it best if you leave."

Highway 26 was relatively free of heavy traffic, but the gas tank was low and they were unable to find a service station that was open. When they finally found one, there was something wrong with the gas pumps and they were delayed even further. It was late when they arrived at the turnoff.

The moon was obscured with heavy clouds and the road from the highway to *Serenity* was dark and ominous. Thick raindrops spattered the windshield and dancing tree branches prophesied an impending storm.

Sam had said little since they left her father's home, and Gordon was deep in thought. The remoteness of the area made her edgy and she broke the silence. "I hope your car's in good condition: I'd sure hate to get stuck out here in this weather."

"Just had it serviced. We'll be okay."

Gordon was forced to throw on his brakes as a deer ran across the road and the sudden deceleration caused the engine to fail. He turned the key. Nothing. Again. Still nothing. "Darn!" he said trying again and again.

"Just had it serviced, huh?"

Gordon didn't answer. He got out of the car, reached into the trunk for a raincoat and put it on. He walked around to the front and lifted the hood. After a moment, he yelled at Sam to try the key again. There was a series of clicks, then silence. Slamming the hood down, he returned to the car and got in. "It's just flooded. It'll start soon."

"How far is it to *Serenity*?" she asked.

"About a mile. I'll walk it, if I have to."

"In this rain? No you won't. Not unless I go, too. You're not leaving me out here alone."

"You don't have a coat and you're in heels: I can make it faster alone. Fischer will loan me a car to come after you. You can lock the doors and I'll leave you my gun."

The rain began to pelt the rooftop. Another five minutes went by and the wind commenced to howl. Wes tried the key;

there was still no response from the engine. He put his hand on the door release but Sam grabbed him by the arm. "No, way, José. You stay with me! Even if we're stuck here all night."

Again he tried the key, but the engine merely coughed and refused to start. "That's it, Kitten; I'm outta here. I'll leave you my gun. Lock the doors and take a nap. Nobody is going to bother you in this rain."

"Wes, I don't want the gun: I wouldn't know what to do with it. Besides, the wrench is more my style."

"Suit yourself. I should be back in half-an-hour." He buttoned his coat around his throat and braved the storm afoot.

Samantha locked the doors, crouched low and tried to keep warm. She began to sing to pass the time. She jolted as a tree branch broke loose and struck the rooftop. She sang louder. *Raindrops are falling on my head*...She envisioned Julie Andrews and the bedroom scene in *The Sound of Music* and she imagined her singing *These Are A Few of My Favorite Things* to her and Cindy.

The storm was getting worse. "I'll sleep," she said aloud. "Time goes by faster." But sleep wouldn't come. She tried to look at her watch, but the night was so dark she couldn't see the hands. She estimated that Wes had been gone for nearly an hour and she wondered what was taking so long. The storm was letting up now and the gentle rain became monotonous. Without trying, she fell asleep.

It was nearly two hours before the rain stopped completely. Samantha was unaware of the time that had passed: she was sound asleep.

Twenty-Nine

He woke out of a bad dream, his head aching. The room was cold and musty and the bed seemed harder than usual. *Covers have fallen to the floor*, he thought as he reached down to grab them. Instead of blankets, he felt concrete. He tried to orient himself, but the room was too dark to see. "Where the devil am I?" he asked bolting upright. He reeled and his head pounded harder. He put his hand to it and felt a lump and a sticky mass. And then he remembered.

He had left Samantha sitting in his car while he jogged the mile to *Serenity* through the storm. He had no trouble getting through the gate—a voice at the intercom let him in with hardly a question. He had sprinted up the steps of the mansion and pressed the doorbell. He remembered that much, but that's it. Except for the hit on the head. As he went down, it felt like someone had dropped a concrete slab on him. That's all he could remember. Until now.

When? What time was it when he left her? Around ten? Or was it eleven? He looked at his watch: the fluorescent hands told him it was 1:20. *A.M. or P.M.? A.M.*, he concluded, *unless there's no window.*

He got up from the bed—a cot with a bare mattress only— and began to inspect his quarters like a blind man. He kicked a bucket and a foul-smelling liquid spilled on his shoes. He struck a wall and followed it around: it was concrete, there were no windows and the air smelled musty. Now, he realized he was in

Fischer's basement. He remembered seeing the room when he was on tour with the Asian.

The room was small—about ten by ten. He found the door, but it was locked—with a deadbolt—and there was no light switch. He felt for his Glock, for the Smith and Wesson and for his cell phone: they were gone.

He reached up and easily touched the ceiling. It was rough wood—boards six inches wide with spaces between. They felt soft and decayed. His hand brushed a light globe dangling from a cord, but there was no pull chain.

They had left him with his clothing. He found his sport coat on the floor at the foot of the cot, picked it up and felt inside the inner pocket. It was there: a Swiss-Army knife Sam had given him when she was just fifteen. The other pockets were stripped bare. Somehow they had missed the pocketknife. "Bless you, Sam," he said softly.

Standing on the cot, he pulled out the longest blade and started chipping away at the boards in the ceiling near the corner of the room; the wood was damp and gave way easily. His progress was slow, but little by little wood chips fell to the floor.

Samantha twisted: it felt like her liver was pinched between her rib and hip. She twisted again and became fully awake. The rain had stopped and the sky was beginning to clear. The moon was generous and allowed her a glimpse at her watch. It was 1:30.

She bolted upright in the seat and looked up the road. "Wesley, where are you? You've been gone three hours!" She started to panic.

Slipping into the driver's seat, she turned the key still in the ignition. Miraculously, the engine coughed, then started. She pressed down on the accelerator and drove slowly along the road looking to the right and to the left as she progressed. She thought of a hundred things that could have happened: he was attacked by a bear, he slipped and hit his head, he got lost. *No, he couldn't get lost. There is only one road and it goes straight to Serenity.* She could see the main gate ahead. *He must have got in, but why hasn't he come back for me?*

She stopped the car a hundred feet from the gate, turned out the headlights and reasoned. *He was right! Mother is in danger—and so is he!*

By moonlight, she backed into a clearing and turned the car around. As soon as she was out of view, she switched the headlights on again and drove away from *Serenity* as fast as she could.

Once on the highway, Samantha began watching for a gas station: there was one just ahead and it was open. She pulled up to the phone booth, found Juan Aguila's phone number listed under *Investigators* and dialed it. His recorder was on, but it gave his home number.

The phone rang several times before he answered. "Yeah, Aguila here. What is it?" he grumbled in a sleepy voice.

"Juan, it's me, Samantha. Wes is in trouble. You've got to come!"

It took nearly an hour of carving before Gordon was able to break away a piece of one-by-six. The flooring above was wet and decayed. *You can thank me for discovering your wet rot, Fischer. Much longer and someone would go right through the floor.* He continued carving and pulling at the wood with his fingers, and eventually had a hole two feet in diameter broken through to the room above. The linoleum was old and thin, and with little effort he cut out a man-sized hole.

He emptied the bucket onto the floor, placed it upside-down on the cot and tried stepping on it to ease himself up through the hole. The bucket tipped and he fell. He tried again and fell again. "This is not going to work...cot's too soft."

Pulling away the mattress, he tipped the cot on its end and leaned it against the wall. Working his feet into the wire mesh, he climbed the cot, eased himself up and through the hole and into the room above.

Through a small window, the moonlight displayed the room's contents. *Laundry room. No wonder there's wet rot.* He started toward the door, but thought about the laundry woman and placed a basket over the hole.

Juan Aguila made good time getting to the gas station. He pulled his Cherokee up next to Sam and got out. It was 2:35 A.M. "Where have you two been? I've been trying all evening to find you."

"I'll tell you while we drive. Let's take your car."

Samantha gave him a detailed account of everything that had occurred that evening. When she finally stopped talking, Aguila let out a low whistle and said, "I could have told you hours ago Corelli and Fischer are partners."

"How do you know that? Who told you?"

"Don't ask. Broke into Corelli's office and went through his files: found correspondence and contracts. The two put up money years ago to buy the old place and renovate it, but Fischer bought him out a couple of years later, then kept him on as a consultant."

Samantha put her hand out to alert him. "We're almost there. Can you drive by moonlight?"

"I've driven with a lot less than that," he said, turning off the headlights. "Now what do we do?"

"I don't know; there's a gate with an intercom. You have to call the office to get through."

"Well, we can't very well do that, can we?"

Aguila drove up to the gate and parked parallel. He jumped out, leaped to the top of the car, then climbed down again and leaned into the car. "I can make it over the fence. When I'm on the other side, drive the car out of sight and wait."

"And sit another three hours? No way. I'm going with you."

"Yeah, sure, I can just see you climbing over that fence in a silk dress and heels. I'll be lucky to make it over myself. Trust me, Samantha, and do as I say."

Reluctantly, Samantha slid into the driver's seat and waited. Aguila picked up a long branch from the roadside and tossed it through the fence. In three jumps, he leaped to the top of the car again, removed his leather jacket and placed it over the gate's spikes. With a strong shove, he hoisted himself over, and then using the branch, he retrieved his coat. "You can go...Wait a minute," he said from the other side. Sam waited. In a moment the gate opened silently.

"How did you do that?" she asked, as he approached her.

"Magic touch. Now, drive the car down the road a ways till it's out of sight. I'll wait here for you."

Except for a soft light near the stairway, the hall was dark. Gordon slipped quietly up the stairs and made his way toward Carla's room. The entire floor was deathly silent until someone called out for a nurse. He ducked into an alcove and waited but lights remained out and the plea for help was left unanswered. Carla's door was just ahead; it was ajar. He slipped through it, moved to her bed and looked down. The bed was stripped. Carla was gone.

Thirty

Aguila guessed the distance from the gate to the mansion to be four hundred feet. Because the area was open and well lit by the moon, and fearing they would be seen, he chose to remain at the periphery near the trees. Samantha's heels dug into the wet grass with each step as they slipped from tree to tree.

The effort to keep her shoes on her feet was slowing them down. "Wait!" she whispered to Aguila as she pulled off her shoes and shoved them into his coat pockets. She stayed close behind him until they reached the rear of the mansion.

"Tell me the layout," he said, stopping short.

"I don't know that much. There's a main lobby around front up the stairs. Sunday I entered through the back door, that way," she said pointing. Sam verbally mapped out the place from her recent encounter and from her memory of visits to her mother during previous years. The information satisfied him and he decided to try entry from the rear.

"Okay, Sam, this is where we part company." Beckoning toward the carriage house, he said, "Stay there till I come for you…"

"Oh, no you don't. You're not leaving me behind. I'm going with you."

"You'll just hold me up."

"That's what Wes said. I'm going."

He could see there was no use arguing, so let her follow. "Okay, but don't sneeze or anything. Any idea where they might have him?"

"Not the faintest," she whispered.

Gordon was baffled. Carla was gone and he had no idea where to start looking. *Call the precinct and report her missing; get backup*, his trained inner voice said. But his common sense told him that could put her in even more danger. He decided to find a phone and call Aguila to pick up Sam—she would still be stranded in her car—and to bring him a weapon. For a brief moment he thought of calling Ballard, but decided against it. It was he who had called Fischer to arrange for his wife to be released. Instead, he got slugged and thrown into the basement. Fischer, for some reason, didn't want his patient released. Maybe Corelli was responsible. There were too many questions that needed answering at this point to trust anyone—even James Ballard. Gordon decided to wait for Aguila before attempting anything heroic—or foolish.

The gate. How would he get him through the gate? The receptionist's desk was the answer. There would be a phone there—and the gate control. He wondered if the Asian was also a night watchman.

Aguila had no trouble picking the lock to the back door: it opened easily and the two slipped in. The interior was dimly lit and there were no sounds coming from any of the rooms they passed by. He tried each doorknob, hoping to find a locked room that might be incarcerating Gordon. They all opened easily and he chanced using a flashlight to explore their contents. There was a kitchen, a pantry, a laundry room, two closets and a breakfast room. One room was inhabited by a fat woman sleeping on a narrow bed and snoring rather loudly. She was unaware of the intrusion. *The housekeeper, no doubt,* thought Aguila.

The next door they tried led down a narrow stairway. "Basement?" whispered Sam.

"Probably. Let's give it a whirl."

It was dark and damp under the house. Thinking of rats and spiders, Sam pulled her shoes from Aguila's pockets and slipped them on. The furnace glowed softly in a distant corner, but afforded little light for them to see by. Aguila turned a switch on his flashlight and it glowed brighter. To the left they could see black earth where the basement had remained unfinished. Three doors led to rooms on the right. Aguila tried the first door: it was a wine closet. Behind the second door was old furniture stacked precariously. The third door was locked.

"Here, hold the flashlight on the lock," he said. He reached into his coat pocket and pulled out the small pick-like instrument he had used earlier on the rear entry door. Inserting it into the lock, he twisted it several times: the lock gave way. Aguila took the flashlight from Sam, opened the door and stepped in. The room was empty except for an overturned bucket and a cot propped upside-down against the wall. Wood chips were scattered on the floor directly below a gaping hole in the ceiling.

"Good show, Gordon," said Aguila. "Now where the heck are you?"

Gordon had no trouble reaching the main lobby without being seen. He questioned the wisdom of keeping the halls so dimly lit in a hospital, but he was grateful for the policy. As he passed by Fischer's office door, he could see light shining beneath it. He ascended the four steps, put his ear to the door and heard soft voices, but couldn't make out what they were saying. Remembering the ivy-covered lattice leading to Fischer's veranda, he decided to let the phone call wait.

Samantha insisted on going to her mother's room. "That's where Wes would go, Juan," she said. "He came here to get her."

"Okay, okay," said the PI. "Show me where it is."

The two ascended the basement stairway again and Sam led him up the central staircase and to her mother's room. The door was open: the bed was empty.

"She's gone!" whispered Sam.

Aguila looked in and saw the stripped bed. The *linens would be there if Gordon has her*, he thought. *Fischer's got her: he's moved her.* He could see from Sam's unnerved expression that she had come to the same conclusion. Grabbing her by the hand, he pulled her out of the room and down the hall. "Come on, kid. We've got to find Gordon." *This place gives me the creeps. And they call it a hospital?*

Climbing the lattice was not easy: it was old and the wood kept breaking. Twice, Gordon slipped and fell to the ground. As he worked his way upward, he wondered why Fischer didn't keep dogs or have a security system. *He's got the Asian. But where is he now?* he thought, puncturing his thumb on a rusty nail near the top. He climbed over the railing and eased himself close to the veranda doors. They were shut tight and drapes prevented him from seeing who was inside, but he was able to hear parts of the conversation through the glass. It had become more heated. He recognized Fischer's voice—it seemed to be directed toward him. The other was too soft to either recognize or understand clearly.

"...should have called me...handled this myself."

"And what would you have done differently?"

"...wouldn't have...was stupid...explain it?"

"Easy. When daylight comes, I'll go down to the basement and apologize. I'll tell him it was Louie: he thought he was a burglar, knocked him out and put him under lock and key till morning. I'll tell him he's been instructed not to disturb me after ten."

"You think...He's no..."

Wes strained to hear what was being said. The voice was still too soft, but he was certain it was a man.

"...do with her?"

"Simple. We had her ready to leave, all packed up and she just disappeared while waiting."

"Yeah, sure...She...over the fence and...."

"No," said Fischer. "We found her later. She'd had an accident. That's why I need time: to make an accident."

"No!" shouted the stranger. "...can't......do it!"

"Hey, we're in this together, up to here. For different reasons, maybe, but we're in it together. I'd have stayed clean, but for you." Fischer began to bellow now. "I did it for you."

The voice shouted back. Now it was loud and shaking with rage. "You did it for the money, you little weasel, and now you blew it! This is the end of your bloodsucking greed, you sniveling little...Hey! No! Rudy, don't..."

There was a muffled shot, then another. Then silence.

Intuitively, Gordon reached for his weapon. It was not there. He was about to charge through the door, but his better judgment prevented it. Instead, he ducked over the railing and climbed down the lattice, the ivy breaking off in his hands as he descended. Near the bottom, he slipped and fell to the ground. As he raised himself from the grass, a hand grabbed him by the shoulder and with little effort pulled him to his feet.

Thirty-One

With one deliberate motion, Gordon elbowed his assailant in the ribs, then swung around and landed a powerful blow to his chin. He prepared himself for a karate chop from the Asian, but there was no return attack. Instead, he found his assailant dazed and lying on the ground. From behind him came a soft but desperate voice.

"Wes, stop! It's Juan!" Samantha grabbed him by the sleeve and pulled him away.

"Good heavens, where did you two come from?" he asked pulling the stunned PI to his feet. "I need a gun. Give me your gun."

"It's in the shop," Aguila mumbled testing his jaw action. "Repairs."

"That's just great! Fischer just wasted someone—Corelli, I think. Then give me your cell phone.

Aguila reached to his pocket. "I must have left it in the car. It's just outside the gate."

"How'd you get through?"

"Smarts, buddy, smarts. Come on."

The three crept through the shadows till they reached the gate. Aguila pressed a button, the gate opened. Impatiently, Gordon held out his hand. "Give me your keys; stay here and hold the gate open. Sam, come with me," he said grabbing her by the arm.

When they reached the car, he jumped in, picked up the phone and called the precinct. He reported the shooting, gave his location and asked for immediate backup without lights and siren. "Call O'Malley and send me a weapon!" he added. Then he ordered Sam into the car. "Stay here, lock the doors and don't move a muscle till this is over. If you see anyone, get to the floor!"

Gordon waited at the gate with Aguila. It seemed like an eternity before three patrol cars pulled up silently. O'Malley was in one. "Where have you been? We've been radioing your car for hours," he said, handing him a gun.

"Indisposed." Gordon told him what had happened. "I don't know who got shot, but I'll bet on Corelli."

"Then let's move in. Gotta plan?"

"Yeah, get there before Fischer disposes of the body."

Gordon briefed the officers and gave them Fischer's description. He and O'Malley headed for the mansion, Aguila and one officer following behind. The remaining officers spread out, covering the grounds.

Gordon vaulted up the steps to the front door and pressed the button. Moments later the porch light went on and a fat woman opened the door. Rubbing her eyes, she said, "Yeah, what do you want?"

"Fischer. Where's Doctor Fischer?" he asked, flashing his badge. Not waiting for a response, he flung the door open, pushed past the woman and across the lobby. O'Malley and Aguila followed; the officer stayed with the woman.

The door of Fischer's office was open; inside it was dark. He fumbled for the light, looked around and said, "This is where he shot Corelli; I was on his veranda."

"How do you know it was Corelli?" the chief asked.

"Who else?" Gordon asked. "See what you can find. I'm going after Fischer." Returning to the lobby, he spoke again to the woman. "Where's the doctor?"

"I don't know; in bed, I guess. Do you want me to wake him?"

"Just tell me where his room is."

The woman pointed up the stairs. "Second door on the right."

Gordon instructed the officer to stay with the woman. He charged up the stairs with gun drawn and flung open the doctor's door. Light from the hall spread across the room. Doctor Fischer sat up in his bed, switched on the bedside lamp and sleepily demanded to know why the interruption.

"Outta bed, Fischer," said the detective. "Where's the body. Where'd you hide it?"

The doctor threw off the covers and swung his feet to the floor. He sat there in his shorts for a moment as if trying to wake up. Running his hands through his carrot-red hair, he stood and shouted, "Sergeant Gordon, you've been watching too many murder mysteries. Would you mind telling me what you're talking about, then get out of my house so I can sleep."

Gordon walked across the room, grabbed him by the shoulder and shoved him toward the door. "It's Lieutenant! I heard the shot, Fischer: I was on your veranda, not locked in the basement, as you thought. You really need to get the termite inspectors out here, you know." Waving his gun toward the stairs, he motioned for the doctor to descend.

"I haven't the faintest idea what you're talking about, *Lieutenant*, and I resent this intrusion. You have no right..."

The detective gave him a shove. "Shut up and move! And I want to know where you're keeping Mrs. Ballard. Now!"

"She's in her room sound asleep, of course."

Gordon turned his suspect over to O'Malley, raced back up the stairs and into Carla Ballard's room. He flicked on the light. She was in her bed, just as Fischer said she would be: the light did not wake her. He walked over to her, placed his hand on her shoulder and shook her lightly: she did not stir. Placing his fingers on her neck, he felt for a pulse: it was slow and barely perceptible. He shook her again, this time more violently, and called her name, but she would not arouse. He returned to the main floor, walked to the receptionist's desk, picked up the phone and requested an ambulance Code Three.

O'Malley was questioning the doctor when an officer came through the front door. "Looks like he threw him from the veranda, Lieutenant. Ivy broken, grass disturbed."

Aguila stepped out of the doctor's office. "And a rug has recently been removed from his office."

"Rug?" broke in Fischer. "You don't know what you're talking about." He turned to O'Malley. "Ask your Lieutenant over there: it was he who messed up my lattice. He admitted he was on my veranda this evening. He should be arrested for violating my property and disturbing the peace!"

Gordon approached the group. "Yeah, and how do you explain this, Fischer?" he said, pointing to the lump on his head. "And my lockup in your basement? Rudy Fischer, I'm arresting you for assaulting a police officer, kidnap and robbery!" Gordon read the doctor his rights, shoved him toward the officer and said, "Take him to the detective division holding cell. And seal off this property with crime scene tape! It may take a while to prove it, but I will. Eventually, I will!"

Thirty-Two

By sun up, *Serenity-In-the Hills* was crawling with police officers, photographers and the media. The few patients who had been committed there were now on their way to a county hospital. Only two employees, the fat woman and her daughter, were found on the grounds: they were in Fisher's office being questioned. The Asian, the receptionist and the nurse who slipped the papers to Gordon the day before had all disappeared. If Fischer had other employees, they, too, had vanished.

Mrs. Ballard was lying in a coma in the intensive care unit at St. Vincent's hospital. She had been so heavily sedated, she would have died within the hour had she not been found and hospitalized. Now, two physicians, three nurses and a room full of highly specialized equipment were struggling to keep her alive.

Samantha was nearby in a phone booth attempting to locate her father: he was nowhere to be found. Nor was Melanie Taylor.

Maria Gonzales Corelli would not cooperate and she refused to admit her husband was missing. *He often goes to the gym when he's troubled. If he's not at his office, he could be almost anywhere.* She promised to call the precinct when he showed up and politely led Gordon to her front door.

As Gordon drove away from the Corelli home, he suspected it was out of fear for her own safety that she refused to answer his questions—or, more likely, she didn't want to incriminate herself. She had insisted that her husband had been at home the entire previous evening and throughout the night and had left an hour before Gordon arrived to go to his office. But when the detective called to verify her story, his secretary said he had not yet arrived.

Gordon had nothing on Maria Corelli, nor on her husband, nothing he could arrest them for—except hunches. He decided to try Samantha. Maybe she could get something out of the woman.

Before returning to *Serenity* to continue the investigation, he stopped at the hospital to check on Mrs. Ballard's condition and to ask Sam to go see Maria. He expected to find James Ballard there by now as well.

"Your dad isn't here yet? It's been hours. Where is he?"

"I call home every ten minutes: he doesn't answer and the recorder's not on. I've tried the bank: they say he hasn't been in nor has he called."

"Have you tried Melanie Taylor?"

"Can't find her. I've tried everyone, Wes. I've even asked Juan to help me locate him."

"How's your Mom?"

"Not good. They think she's been poisoned. It wasn't just the Valium."

Under the circumstances, Gordon hesitated to ask Sam to go to Maria's house—he knew she would want to remain with her mother—and at this point, finding Mr. Ballard was more important. He was convinced Corelli's body would turn up sooner or later, and that would undoubtedly bring Maria to her knees. She would confess her part in the scheme and implicate both her husband and Fischer in the telling.

Gordon gave Samantha a fatherly hug and told her to keep her chin up. "I'll be at *Serenity*. Let me know if her condition changes—or if they identify the poison. It will be one more thing we can hang on Fischer. And call me the minute you locate your father."

As he approached *Serenity*, he saw a myriad of reporters and photographers arguing with an officer who was guarding the entrance to the grounds. Two television vans and a number of cars partially obstructed the way. Slowly, he maneuvered his vehicle between them, drove up to the crime scene tape that was stretched across the entrance and stopped.

One of the reporters recognized him and within seconds, microphones were being shoved in his face. Had he been able to get a confession out of Dr. Fischer? How was Mrs. Ballard? Have the remains that were dug up been identified yet? Is there any evidence that Cynthia Ballard might still be alive? Did they know who had been shot?

"I heard a shot. That's all I can tell you," he said. The officer released the tape and he drove through. *Vultures! Preying on the privacy of people's lives! And someday Sam will be one of them!*

A warrant had been secured for access to Fischer's private records and a detective was searching through his files when Gordon entered the doctor's office. The detective turned and Gordon recognized him: it was Wade Thornton, recently promoted to Sergeant. "Just got transferred to homicide," he said. "O'Malley thought you could use a hand."

Gordon objected to the unexpected assistance on the investigation, but knew O'Malley well enough to accept the help without argument. Till now, the chief had allowed him to go it alone since the investigation had been suspended pending new leads, but now it was murder. Gordon suspected Thornton was to be his new partner.

"Appreciate any help I can get. How much do you know about the case?" Gordon asked.

"Only what O'Malley told me, which wasn't much. He said you'd be needing a warrant to go through Fischer's records so I wrote the affidavit and Judge Turner signed it." Thornton held up a key. "Got this from Fischer: showed him the warrant and asked if he wanted me to break into his files or if he preferred not to have them repaired. He gave me the key."

Good thinking, thought Gordon as he surveyed the man. He was tall, slender and muscular. His skin was black and his head was as bald as an eagle's. Across his left cheek was a scar that extended from just under his eye to his jaw. It looked like a recent injury that had not yet fully healed. "Found anything yet?"

Thornton handed over a bank statement. "Not much, but this is interesting."

Gordon took a look and pursed his lips into a long, low whistle. "Two-hundred fifty-five thousand in a simple checking account? Doesn't the guy know he'd get better interest from a CD?"

"Maybe he's thinking of writing a check?" added Thornton.

"Maybe," Gordon agreed. He thumbed through the pages and noticed that most of the balance had been deposited to the account during the past month. "Keep looking, Thornton. You might come up with something. I'll fill you in later on what we've got." He walked away thinking it might be okay to have a partner that wasn't gun shy. His former partner quit the force after realizing he could never pull the trigger.

Before he left the room, he turned and looked again at the scar on Thornton's cheek. "Where'd you get the souvenir?" he asked touching his own cheek.

"My wife," was the answer.

As he left the room, an officer approached. "Lieutenant, we found a road out back. It's concealed with artificial shrubs. Fresh tire tracks, too."

"Where? Take me to it. Where does it go?"
"Officer Baker is following it now. Should be back soon."
"Are they casting the tracks?"
"Doing that now, sir."

Gordon followed the officer through the building to the back door and across the lawn. A hundred feet beyond the guesthouse, they had found a narrow road that led into the forest and up the mountainside. Its entry was cleverly camouflaged with artificial shrubs attached to a base that swung freely from an iron post, also camouflaged with vines.

"Clever," admitted Gordon, kicking at the post with his right foot. "But people don't go to all this trouble unless they have something to hide. Let's see what it is."

The officer followed Gordon up the road and watched him as he methodically probed the ground and examined the brush. Except for an occasional hint of sunlight piercing through the dense trees, the way was dark and damp. The storm had muddied the road and two sets of fresh tire tracks were distinctly visible. Officers were busily casting them.

"Get pictures?" asked Gordon.

"Yes, sir, both sets."

"Good work. They must have driven through here after the storm." *And after the shot. The ground had a chance to dry somewhat.* "How long ago did Baker leave? On foot, I presume."

"Yes, sir. Didn't want to disturb the tracks. Been gone about half-an-hour."

The two men continued exploring the roadside and looking for footprints leading from the road into the woods until Gordon was convinced that a thorough search of the area should be ordered. *A body could have been buried up here: a great place to bury someone*, he mused. He turned to go back to the hospital.

"Lieutenant Gordon!" It was Baker, returning from his jaunt. "I found the outlet. The road heads back downhill farther up. It comes out onto Shady Grove Lane."

"Can we approach it from the main road?"

"Didn't walk that far, but I suspect so."

Gordon and Officer Baker drove down the mountainside to the main road and headed west looking for Shady Grove Lane. They found it a couple of miles away. Baker turned right into the lane and continued another mile before he stopped the car and pointed. "This is where it comes out, Lieutenant. Want me to drive in?"

"Not yet," answered the detective as he climbed from the car and ambled up the narrow, dirt road. The sun had dried the mud, but two sets of tire tracks were still clearly visible. He stooped and examined them more closely. *Same as the other end,* he decided. "Okay, let's go up," he said, returning to the car.

Baker drove slowly trying to avoid the ruts. The road was narrow—barely wide enough for one car—and at times, brush extended from one side to the other. They drove on until it began to weave in and out among the alders and then through the pines. Soon they were in dense forest and were headed downhill again. Another half mile and they reached the point where Gordon had met Baker an hour earlier.

"Stop the car. I'll walk from here. You go ahead," said Gordon as he opened the door.

Baker drove on.

Gordon walked slowly down the road searching for evidence: footprints, anything that might indicate a body had been dragged through the trees. He found nothing.

They'll find him, he assured himself. *Later, when we get a team out here, they'll find Corelli.* Smug with self-confidence, Gordon headed for the camouflaged entrance. When he reached the clearing, he saw Juan Aguila headed his way. Frantically, he was waving some papers in his hand. *He's found something,* thought Gordon. *Something important.*

Thirty-Three

Carla Ballard had the will to live on. Even in her highly debilitated state, she refused to die. Medical science and the skills of her physicians were an adjunct to her recovery, but it was Carla's inner strength that kept her alive.

"By all rights, your mother should be gone now, Ms. Ballard. But it takes more than what we have to offer to bring someone back when they are that far gone. She must have been endowed with that special something most people don't have; she must have been fighting to stay with us, even in a comatose state." The doctor was still shaking his head as he walked from the room.

Samantha stood by her mother's bedside and held her hand while nurses checked tubes that seemed to grow from her body cavities. Lights on the machines to which she was attached blinked in rhythm with the sounds that emitted as the functioning of her frail and damaged organs failed to improve.

She had suffered tremendous abuse and overdose from sedatives. They alone should have killed her and were doing so gradually, but someone apparently saw the need for her sudden demise and had administered a potent and lethal poison. Whoever gave it had selected one that would be quick and unidentifiable. And it would have been just that had it not been for the astute observation of Katherine Oberly, the crime lab's senior criminalist.

Katy, as she was called, had gone through the Academy at Monmouth long before Gordon was on the scene and knew the ropes as well as any officer on the force. She had put in her time on the streets, behind the desk and in the black-and-whites for twelve years before she decided to become a criminalist. And she was the best. She had a sixth sense that had cracked more cases than any of them so it was not surprising that she would contribute to solving this one.

She and her assistant were at *Serenity* collecting evidence in an attempt to prove a crime had been committed when the lab called. The doctors treating Mrs. Ballard suspected poisoning since they found vomitus and diarrheal stool on her body, but they were helpless, not knowing what antidote to give, and time was running out. The lab had already received a sample of Mrs. Ballard's blood and urine and they had isolated an organic compound but were unable to identify it.

Immediately, Katy, her assistant and two officers went to work in search of something lethal that might have been administered to Carla Ballard. Moments later, as Katy was scanning the patient's room, she noticed a leaf under the bed. Wheels turned in her head. She grabbed the leaf, flew down the stairs to Dr. Fischer's office and barged through the doors to the veranda. As she suspected, the leaf matched those from the rhododendron plant that encroached upon the railing.

Inside, she grabbed the phone from Dr. Fischer's desk and dialed the hospital. "This is the Portland Crime Lab calling," she said to the operator that answered. "Put me through to Intensive Care. It's an emergency."

The nurse who answered transferred the call to Mrs. Ballard's physician.

"It's rhododendron," she said. "Maybe. I don't know for sure. It's like foxglove. Test her for digitalis toxicity."

Carla Ballard's heart monitor showed the characteristic extreme ECG changes consistent with digitalis poisoning, but the chart that had come with her from *Serenity* did not indicate she was on the drug. The doctors would not have suspected it, had it not been for the phone call.

Immediately, the patient's blood was tested for digitalis toxicity and serum levels were high. Since her cardiac monitor showed low potassium levels, she was started immediately on intravenous potassium chloride. Gradually, her condition improved.

"What made you think of rhododendron poisoning?" Katy's assistant asked later.

"My dog. He chewed up my rhody plant a few months ago and got really sick—almost died. But I really give the credit to my mother-in-law: she used to try all sorts of new teas. One time I caught her about to drink a tea made from rhododendron leaves: she insisted it would be good for her arthritis. I stopped her just in time. Had to bring a book home from the lab to prove it was poison. She wouldn't take my word for it."

The assistant was still curious. "But a leaf under a bed. Whatever made you think it was the cause?"

"There were no flowers in the room. I checked the wastebasket and found a few more leaves there. And there was a cup in her bathroom. The suspect had dumped the contents but didn't wash it out."

Juan Aguila approached Gordon with the papers still fluttering in his hand. His right leg was dragging somewhat—more than usual—and Gordon knew he'd been over-using it. A flash of guilt passed through him as he strode quickly across the lawn to meet the PI.

"Okay, so what you got?" questioned Gordon.

"Ballard. He was flying out this morning. Take a look at this." Aguila handed him two plane tickets to Mexico City: departure time was thirty minutes ago. The tickets were made out to James Ballard and Melanie Taylor.

"Where'd you get these?"

"From Ballard's desk. Sam wanted me to find him: I figured the best place to start was where she'd last seen him—at home. She gave me the key to his house. They were right there in plain sight lying on the desk."

"What else?"

"A lot more. A bag was on his bed, half filled with clothing..."

"And?" Gordon was anxious. Aguila wasn't talking fast enough.

"And so I checked with the airlines. He made the reservations yesterday morning."

"That's what I wanted to hear. Juan, you've got to find Melanie Taylor. She'll..."

The PI stopped him. "I found her. She's waiting in my car."

Samantha Ballard smiled as she gently squeezed her mother's hand. Her breathing was stronger now and the cardiac monitor was sending a message of a regular heart rhythm. She hadn't opened her eyes yet, but she knew someone was there: she was trying to speak.

Sam leaned forward and put her ear close to her mouth. "What it is, Mother? What are you trying to say?"

"...home...Cindy...home..."

"I understand, Mom. We're going to take you home as soon as you're better. You're going to get better now."

"...Cindy..."

Samantha straightened up and stared at the ailing woman who had given her birth. She longed to hold her, to be able to call her *Mother* and be recognized as a daughter again, to hear her say *Samantha*, instead of Cindy—just once. If only she could hear her call her name...

It was happening. Sam recognized the strange feeling that always preceded a premonition. *Not now,* she thought. *Not now, please.* But it was too late.

Eyes closed, she tilted her head back and let it sway to and fro as the pounding began. Unexplained energy seemed to flow from her mother's hand to hers and into her body. She grew hot and began to perspire. And then she saw her sister. She was with Maria Gonzales: they were arguing. Cindy was not a child this time: she was an adult with short, dark, curly hair.

"Okay, Fischer, let's try again: Where'd you hide Corelli's body?" Chief O'Malley's nose was turning red. He'd been with the doctor for thirty minutes this time, trying to break him. The man stayed calm and quiet, his response always the same: *I don't know what you're talking about.*

"Look, you little…"

The chief's expletive was interrupted. An officer said he was wanted on the phone. It was Gordon calling from St. Vincent's.

"We've got him, Chief: it was rhododendron. He made her a tea with the leaves—it's deadly."

"Did she die?"

"Nope, she's going to make it. They caught it just in time. And we can thank Katy for that one."

The chief shifted the phone to the other ear. "Could have been anyone. Maybe she made the tea herself."

"Maybe. The cup is on its way to the lab. I'll bet you a week's slave labor without pay they'll find tea residue and Fischer's fingerprints on it. Get anything out of him?"

"Not yet."

"I'm coming in. Aguila struck gold; we're looking for the wrong guy."

"What do you mean—wrong guy?" asked the chief.

"I'll tell you when I get there." Gordon hung up and headed back to Intensive Care.

Juan Aguila and Melanie Taylor were waiting for him just outside the door.

"Where's Sam?" Gordon asked, looking around for her.

"She took off," the PI said. "She and Melanie talked and she left. She never said where she was going, but she asked for Corelli's address."

Gordon looked at Melanie and received a blank stare. "What did you talk about?" he asked.

"Her father. I told her the truth about her father."

Thirty-Four

Gordon steered Juan Aguila and Melanie Taylor into the hospital meditation room. He closed the door and led her to the sofa. "You told Sam the truth about her father. Now tell me."

Melanie sat down, folded her hands neatly in her lap and stared at the crucifix on the wall opposite them. "I...I don't know where to start. I..."

"Start at the beginning," Gordon said, sitting beside her.

"It goes back a long way."

"We've got plenty of time."

Not wanting to detract from the blonde's confession, Aguila took a seat across the room.

The woman swallowed the lump in her throat and began. "I knew Jim long before he married Carla. We went to school together; we were very close then." She paused, as though reminiscing about the past. "We lost track of each other when he went away to college. It wasn't until after he and Carla were married that we ran into each other. I was at the bank applying for a loan when he saw me. We went to lunch..."

Gordon interrupted. "Do you remember when that was?"

"Yes, because he mentioned he and Carla had just had twins. He showed me their picture: they were two weeks old." Melanie shifted her position and continued. "I didn't see much of him during the next three or four years, other than at the bank, of course. Then one day..." She paused.

"Go on," urged Gordon.

"One day, he called me. He was very upset and wanted to see me. We met at a little restaurant downtown: we talked about Carla, his wife."

"About Carla? What about Carla?"

"She no longer wanted him."

"What do you mean?"

"I mean sexually. He said all she could think about was the twins."

"And so you filled the need..."

"No! No, I didn't, not then. I tried to help him find the reason for her disinterest. I told him it might be his fault. I didn't want to break up a home."

"And?"

"We remained friends, met occasionally for lunch, then I didn't see him for awhile."

"How long was *awhile*?"

"Two years, maybe more. Then one day I ran into Carla. I had never met her before, but I had seen them together so knew who she was. We were at Nordstrom's looking at the same dress. We started talking and I liked her. I liked her very much." Melanie stood up and walked to the water fountain. When she returned, there were tears in her eyes. "I never wanted to hurt her!"

"But you couldn't help yourself."

"Yes, no! Jim was very persistent. Not long after that we began seeing each other again. He seemed very disturbed about something. I thought I could help."

"Go on."

"One day he came to me..."

"To your house?"

"Yes, to my house. He came with a lot of money—cash, in a briefcase. He wanted me to keep it for him."

"Did he say where he got it?"

"No, he just asked me to hold it for him."

"How much?"

Melanie Taylor gulped. "Twenty thousand dollars."

Gordon was taken back, but not wanting to distract her train of thought, he remained calm and let her continue.

"I wondered where he got it, but he never offered to tell me." Lowering her voice, she continued, haltingly. "A couple of months later...he brought the briefcase again."

Aguila was straining to hear. Gordon leaned forward. "With more money?" he asked.

Melanie hesitated. "Yes, but this time he had fifty-thousand."

"How often did this happen?"

"Over the next year or so? Four...No, five times."

"Where did you keep the money?"

"In the attic. That's where he put it."

"You weren't afraid of a fire?"

The distraught woman wrung her hands and answered, "He kept it in a fireproof box."

"I see. Then what?"

Shifting her position, she continued her story, less reluctant now to tell it. "After a year or so, he said he wanted to invest it. By then, I was in real estate and he thought I could help."

"You weren't curious as to where he got it?"

"Oh, yes, he told me he was embezzling it from the bank."

Gordon shot up from the sofa. The thought had crossed his mind, but he was stunned that she would admit it so readily—as if embezzlement was the fashionable thing to do. "And you went along with it, just like that?"

"I had no choice. I was an accessory to the fact."

"But you could have come to us! You'd have got off."

"No, it wasn't that easy: he had used me to help in the embezzling, you see. It was through my account that he altered the books somehow. He convinced me I would be convicted right along with him if he were found out."

"And you were in love with him."

"Yes, I think so. I'm not sure."

Gordon had never in sixteen years heard a confession that came so easily. It unnerved him. "Did you tell Samantha this?"

"Goodness, no!"

"Then what did you tell her? You said you told her the truth about her father."

"I did, but not this. I told her about the plane tickets, that we were leaving the country. And that she would find a quitclaim deed to the house in his desk drawer. That's all."

"That's all?"

"And that he had deposited fifty-thousand to her account."

"But you never mentioned he had been embezzling money."

"No, I couldn't bring myself to tell her that. I couldn't hurt her that way."

"And that's when she left?"

"Yes."

"Do you know where she went?"

"No, all she said was, *Now, I know why he wrote the letter.* She mumbled something about *Maria*, asked Juan for her address and took off quite suddenly."

Gordon was overwhelmed. "Why are you telling me this now? Why not yesterday—or the day before?"

"Because Jim never showed up at the airport. He wouldn't have left me standing there like that, I know. Besides, I had the money. I think something terrible has happened to him."

Sam had intended to go straight to Maria's house and confront her, but the news of her father running away to Mexico with Melanie Taylor held her back. She had to be alone first, to sort out the facts, to vindicate his actions. And to prepare herself for the inevitable when the DNA matched her blood with those of the remains the police dug up.

Samantha drove into the hills and parked at a viewpoint. Tears clouded the scene as she looked out over the valley. She brushed them away, but they returned. Why would he leave without an explanation? she asked herself. Was he that much in love with Melanie? Was it because her mother was coming back and he wanted to escape the responsibility of caring for her again? No, there had to be a better reason. But what was it? Maybe if she had taken the letter more seriously and stayed in Seattle, maybe then...

The tears had dried now; she could see more clearly and she knew what she had to do. The valley below was shrouded and still except for the tiny, ant-like string of cars on the highway. She slipped from the car and walked to the edge of the viewpoint. She looked down and the angel of death reached out for her, telling her to take one more step. She stood motionless for a moment, but turned, lifted her head high and walked back to her car. Her mother needed her and the house needed preparation.

She was ready to go to Maria now. It was time to confront her, to convince her that she must tell the truth.

Thirty-Five

Lieutenant Wesley Gordon was just handed another piece to the puzzle: Melanie Taylor had supplied it. It fit in very nicely and confirmed his suspicions.

"I'm going to have to take you in, Ms. Taylor. You understand why, don't you?"

The woman nodded. "Will you find Jim?"

"Yes, we'll find him. It may take awhile, but I think I know where he is." The detective read the troubled woman her rights and the three left the hospital.

Gordon eased the woman into the backseat of his car and closed the door. He turned to Juan Aguila and placed his hand on his shoulder. "You done good, man. You always were a step ahead of me."

"Not by a long shot, ol' buddy. Just did my job. Speaking of my job, what do I do with the information I got from Davies? And a suitcase full of hundred dollar bills?"

"Hah! We could buy my sloop!" replied the detective.

"Or a yacht." Aguila slapped him on the back. "Walk me to my car and I'll turn it over to you."

"Yeah." Gordon glanced at his prisoner who seemed quite content to remain where she was. He followed the PI to his car parked a short distance from his.

"You know something you're not telling me," said Aguila.

"I want to be sure. You'll be the first to know when I know. Brief me on what you learned from Davies."

Aguila unlocked the trunk of his car, pulled out a manila envelope and a small suitcase. "The money," he said. "Go buy your sloop. And here's the file Davies sent me—it's self-explanatory. It'll answer some questions."

Gordon led Melanie Taylor into the precinct and placed her in an interview room. "I'll be with you in ten," he said. "You won't object to being recorded, will you?"

"Do I have a choice?"

"Not really. But you did the right thing: they'll go easy on you for it. Are you sure you don't want to call your attorney?"

"I don't have one; I just want to get this over with so you can find Jim."

Rudy Fischer, M.D. was stretched out on the cot in a holding cell. Gordon unlocked the door and let himself in. Fischer didn't move, nor did he speak.

"Looks like we've got you all tied up in a nice little package, Dr. Fischer. You should have washed out the cup at least, especially since you left your fingerprints on it."

Fischer remained silent.

"But you're lucky. You'll get sent up for one murder, not two. Mrs. Ballard is going to pull through. As a matter of fact, she's starting to speak quite coherently. It'll be interesting to hear what she has to say when she tells us all about *Serenity*—and you—and Dr. Corelli."

Fischer rolled over and faced the wall.

"You don't have to talk now. We found your secret little road: they're searching the woods at this very moment. It's just a matter of time and we'll find the body." Gordon moved closer and tapped him on the shoulder. "You're not very smart, you know, keeping all that money in your checking account. And making tea from rhododendron, that's dangerous stuff, Fischer. You might have slipped and drunk it yourself." Gordon paused to see if there was a response, but Fischer didn't move, so he went on. "Oh, yes, and you should have listened to Mrs. Ballard about the trees. It's a shame to see them being chewed up that way when they could have been sprayed."

Fischer turned and glared at the detective.

Gordon smiled superficially, then turned and walked out. Before closing the door, he said, "I'm curious about one thing though. How did you manage to get rid of the Hertz Rental agent? That one still puzzles me."

Melanie Taylor repeated her confession once more for the recorder. There was nothing she could add to what she told Gordon at the hospital, nor did she leave anything out. Ballard had used her: perhaps he was in love with her, but he had used her as well.

It was quite obvious that she knew nothing about the kidnapping beyond what the general public knew. It only fed her capacity to empathize with *the poor man*, as she called him.

Gordon apologized for having to detain her—he truly felt sorry for the woman—and turned her over to the officer in charge. "Make her comfortable," he said. "She's got a big shock coming up."

O'Malley was leaning back in his big chair with his hands clasped behind his head and a grin that stretched from ear to ear when Gordon walked in. The suitcase Aguila had turned over to him was open on top of his desk: it was filled with neatly stacked hundred dollar bills.

"You look like you just won the lottery. What's up?" Gordon asked.

"No, you won it, Lieutenant," he said, grinning even wider. "They just found the body."

Thirty-Six

Samantha drove around the block twice before she felt prepared to challenge Maria. Having gained confidence, she stopped in front of her house to rehearse her speech one last time. She would not accuse her of kidnapping her sister. She had been trained to interview: she would use the techniques of a news reporter. And then, little by little, probe her responses until she slipped and revealed herself.

Sam was ready; it was time. As she was removing her keys from the ignition, the garage door of Maria's house slid upward and a white Cadillac Seville drove in. The door closed again before she could see who was in the car.

Sam froze. Could it be Dr. Corelli? *No, he is dead*, she reminded herself. *Dr. Fischer shot him. They are searching for his body this very moment. It has to be Maria.*

Before she could regain her confidence, the garage door flew open once more. In the shadows, she saw a woman hurriedly climb into the Seville. It was Maria. The engine started and she backed out barely missing the center post. In her flight, she forgot to close the garage door.

Sam watched the car careen around the corner and disappear from view. *Too late*, she thought. *She's gone! I've missed her!*

But the garage door stood open, inviting her in.

Sam slipped from her car, scanned the neighborhood for busybodies, but saw no one. Quickly, she strode across the street, entered the garage and tried the inside door: it opened into a hallway. Listening for voices and hearing no one, she stepped inside.

She walked into the living room, surveyed the decor and furnishings, and silently pronounced them ostentatious. *Not like Maria,* she thought. *She was always modest and humble. He has changed her.*

She explored the kitchen and found nothing that might implicate the Corellis. But a tiny red light blinked on the telephone answering machine and she could not resist the temptation to listen to its message. She touched the button.

Maria, where have you been? I need you—now! Someone has gone through the files and the police have arrested Fischer. Don't tell Lisa; just get in here!

It was a man's voice. It can't be Dr. Corelli, she thought. Dr. Fischer shot him; he's dead!

She shut off the machine. Impulsively, she removed the tape and slipped it into her handbag.

As she wandered through the house, the message continued to play over in her mind. Who could have left the message? And who is Lisa?

The grandfather's clock in the hallway chimed and Sam bolted. It was 11:30 A.M. She was beginning to feel uneasy, but she couldn't bring herself to leave.

After going through a desk in the den and finding nothing that might incriminate the Corellis, Samantha approached the stairway. Still nervous and undecided about continuing the search, she put her hand on the stair railing and looked up. She was about to forego the second floor when her hand became warm. She lifted it from the railing and the warmth diminished. Again, she laid it on the railing and the warmth returned. She could feel Cindy's presence somewhere in Maria's house!

Wes Gordon punched the air above him with a clenched fist and let out a yelp. "I knew it! It was just a matter of time." With feet spread wide and hands slapped upon O'Malley's desk, he eyeballed his superior and bellowed, "It's not Corelli, is it?"

"Corelli? Sure it is...You said...we don't know yet, Gordon. They dug up a body—that's all I know!"

Gordon spun on his heel and headed towards the door. "It's not Corelli! I'll bet you a month of Sunday dinners it's not Corelli!"

The chief shouted out, "Then who...Gordon, come back here!" It was too late: the detective had disappeared down the hall toward the elevator.

He made it to *Serenity* in record time and pulled through the gate just as Harry was getting out of his car. He called for him to wait and the two walked together to the wooded area where officers had unearthed the corpse. Katy was there—and Thornton, giving instructions.

It was wrapped in a rug too small to completely conceal both head and feet. After photos and measurements had been taken and Katy had given the okay, the officers lifted it from its shallow grave.

Slowly, they unrolled a bloodstained rug that Gordon recognized as one that had been in Fischer's office. More pictures were taken and then two officers carefully rolled the body into a supine position. Gordon was not surprised when he saw the face: he knew it would not be Corelli. As he expected, it was the body of a man he had known well for eleven years. It was James Ballard!

Gordon's first thought was of Samantha. Somehow, after talking with Melanie, he knew Fischer had killed Sam's father, not Corelli, as he first presumed. And he knew why. But how would he ever be able to explain it to Sam. She had lost a sister, had almost lost her mother, and now she had lost her father.

It would be more than she could bear. But the reason for her father's death would be devastating.

He looked at his watch. It was almost noon and he had been up all night. It seemed like days since he'd been slugged and thrown in Fischer's basement: a lot had happened since then. It was time now to find Samantha and prepare her for another shock. He would let someone else tell Melanie Taylor.

She had probably gone to the Corelli home. He wondered how she knew where they lived, but then he remembered Aguila had given her the address.

Harry and Katy were hovered over the body. This was their department: he wouldn't be needed now. And Thornton knew homicide; he could handle the wrap up. And the reporters.

Gordon said goodbye and walked away. No one noticed he had gone.

Thirty-Seven

For years Samantha had resisted any notion that her sister was dead, but now the feeling of Cindy's presence was stronger than ever: she *knew* she was alive. She stood at the foot of the stairs gazing upward, straining to catch the sound of a voice or the shuffling of feet. She heard nothing but the pounding of her own heart. She started up the steps. A drop of perspiration slithered down her forehead. She wiped it away with the back of her hand and paused to calm herself. Taking a deep breath, she courageously took another step. And another.

The hall was dark at the top of the stairs. She groped for a light switch. Finding it, she flicked it on. The glow helped her gain confidence and she started down the hall. The first door stood open. It was a small room that held a cabinet, a bookcase and a table with a sewing machine that was still warm. The tiny light illuminated the colorful fabric that spilled onto the floor. It was as if someone had stepped out for a snack or to answer the door. She reached over and touched the soft material. As she fingered it, she felt the presence of Cindy again. *Cindy is here. Cindy was sewing.* Her heart raced with excitement as her hopes grew.

Compulsively, Sam turned out the little light and left the room. The sensation became stronger as she continued her tour, pausing and listening at each closed door. At the end of the hall, she touched the last doorknob. It felt warm and her hand tingled and she knew someone was inside. *Cindy*, she thought. *It has to* be *Cindy*. She turned the knob slowly and gradually inched it open.

The drapes were drawn and the room was darkened, but Sam could see someone lying across the bed face down, her arm curled under her head to make a pillow, her face turned away from the door.

Sam's throat tightened. She felt herself drawn towards the still body. Softly, she called out, "Cindy?"

The sleeping figure did not move. At that moment, she heard someone coming up the steps.

Triumphant, yet defeated, Lieutenant Gordon climbed into his car with as much enthusiasm as a slug in drought. Ten minutes earlier, he was congratulating himself for being so clever. Now, he wanted to crawl into a hole and close out the world. It was a rough life, dealing day in and day out with scumbags like Rudy Fischer and the Corellis.

And James Ballard.

It hadn't really hit him until now what Ballard had done to his family. He had suspected him the night he and Aguila were at his apartment hashing it out over pizza. He didn't want it to be Ballard. And yet, he couldn't bring himself to take his name off the suspect list.

It still doesn't add up, he mused. *Why would Ballard kidnap his own kid!*

He slammed the car door and started the ignition. Not wanting to go to Samantha, he turned the engine off and sat there thinking. And wondering how so much garbage could evolve out of what at one time was thought to be a simple kidnap case.

"Simple?" he said aloud, turning the key in the ignition. "Not so simple. All this, and we still haven't got solid evidence on who kidnapped and murdered Cindy."

He slammed his foot on the gas pedal and pulled out of the parking lot. Driving down the mountain road, he fabricated motives—starting with Fischer. He could have rented the car, but did he abduct the child? No, he did it for Corelli. Or Ballard. Or Maria. Which? Maybe he didn't even know why they wanted the car. Maybe he was clean back then. Or, maybe they were all in it together. At a curve, he let up on the gas pedal.

Motive. He needed a motive.

"Think. Think," he said, as he pounded his forehead with his knuckles.

Then it struck him. It was something that came to him out of the blue, something Samantha had said several days earlier that hit him.

At a corner, he stopped to digest the concept.

Yes. Maybe. Yes! He slammed his foot hard on the gas pedal and sped off. He had his motive. And maybe the kidnapper, too. Now, all he had to do was to prove it.

Gordon grabbed his cell phone and dialed the precinct. He asked for the detail clerk. "Annie, I need your help ASAP," he said. "Have LEDS run me a criminal history on James Ballard—middle initial is T. He's the homicide they're bringing in now. And when they've got prints, have them run in WIN. I want everything you can dig up on the guy as far back as you can go. Copy?"

"Got it, Lieutenant, how soon do you need it?"

"Yesterday! Call me on my cell phone the minute you've got something."

Thirty-Eight

Maria! She thought, as Samantha looked for a place to hide. As the steps came closer, Samantha slipped into a closet and hid behind the clothing. Through the half open door she saw a small, black woman step into the room. The woman moved to the bed and stood over the sleeping figure. Quietly, she removed something from her handbag, paused, and then in a deep, husky voice said, "It's time for your shot, Lisa. Pull up your sleeve."

Immediately, Samantha reacted. She knew who this woman was and she feared the injection might be lethal! Stepping out of the closet, she searched for a weapon but found nothing before the woman turned and saw her. It was too late. With one quick twist of her body, the woman's leg shot out and clipped Samantha in the abdomen. Sam folded and dropped to the floor in pain.

The black woman fell upon the bed and aimed the needle at her patient. But she missed.

Sam saw her face. It was Cindy!

"Jessie, what are you doing here? Who let you in? Who's that girl on the floor?" Cindy had become fully alert during the commotion and had moved at the very moment the black woman was about to give her the shot. Instantly, she jumped from the bed and stood defensive.

Sam was still doubled up in pain, her head bowed, but she rolled into the closet to avoid another attack. The black woman followed her, now aiming the needle her direction, but she was disarmed when Cindy threw a pillow at her. The syringe flew from Jessie's hand.

Sam recovered, seized a shoe and threw it directly at the woman's head. Her aim was perfect! The heel found its mark at the woman's left temple and she reeled. It gave Sam just the time she needed to grab a pair of scissors that were lying on the dresser and plunge them deep into the woman's shoulder. Blood spurted and the woman slumped to the floor.

Cindy stared in horror. She remained frozen until Samantha spoke.

"Cindy, it's me, Samantha."

"I'm not Cindy. My name is Lisa. And who are you?" she shouted, still shaking. But she couldn't take her eyes off this intruder who looked exactly like herself.

The wounded woman groaned. Sam whipped about, saw her victim reach out for her ankle, but she jumped from her reach.

"Lisa," shouted Jessie, "she's here to hurt you! Help me!"

Cindy was confused. Dr. Fischer's receptionist had never come to the Corelli home before. And who was this stranger who looked like her? But she was drawn to her. Instantly, she made a decision. "I don't know who you are, but I think we'd better call an ambulance before Jessie bleeds to death."

"She was going to give you a shot, Cindy! I think she was going to kill you!"

"My name is Lisa! Lisa Kendall! Why would she want to kill me?" Cindy threw a blouse at Sam. "Stay here and apply pressure to her wound, or you might be up for murder!"

"Wait! It's the police we need to call! Tell them..." It was no use. Cindy had left the room. Sam dropped to the floor and pressed the blouse into the bleeding wound of the woman who was now unconscious.

How ironic, she thought, *that her sister would be discovered in this manner*. The twins had just saved each other's life and

Cindy didn't even know who she was. Lisa Kendall? The name sounded familiar.

Then Sam remembered.

Her mind flashed back. She heard the husky voice through the intercom at the hospital. *Sorry, Miss Kendall. I didn't see you drive up.* And the message on the recorder had said, *Don't tell Lisa.* So they had even given her a new name. That's why Sam was allowed to leave the hospital grounds the day she had sneaked in to visit her mother: the receptionist thought she was Cindy—or rather, Lisa. Apparently, her sister had the freedom to come and go from the hospital as she pleased.

Then it became clear. It was all a clever but stupid plan. Maria loved Cindy and wanted her for herself. She kidnapped her. But she botched the job when the car went off the road so never had a chance to pick up the ransom money. She never intended to return Cindy to her family. It was revenge for being fired. Their father was right! Maria was not to be trusted. To be sure Cindy would not want to return to her home, Dr. Corelli drugged her with something that would erase the memory of her family from her mind, just as they had done to the twins' mother. Being a psychiatrist, he would know just what to use.

And maybe their mother discovered what had happened and was going to inform the police. That had to be why they kept her captive all these years.

Samantha's head was swimming. The whole picture was coming together like a puzzle, each piece fitting into place. She was so deep in thought, she didn't notice someone had entered the room. It was Maria.

Maria rushed to the unconscious woman, pushed Sam aside and inspected the wound. She turned to Sam and said, "She's okay—the bleeding has stopped." She yanked the scarf from her neck, wrapped it tightly around the woman's shoulder, then pulled some rope from her pocket and bound the woman to the bedpost. "Well, Samantha, I never thought we would meet again under such circumstances. How did you get in?"

"You left the garage door open. It was easy."

"It looks like we have a lot of explaining to do. But first, I think we should dispose of Jessie."

"Kill her? Like Dr. Fischer did to your husband?"

"Dr. Fischer didn't kill my husband. And, no, I don't mean kill her, I mean get her to the hospital—she needs treatment. How's your mother?"

Maria was gently slapping Jessie's face. She was beginning to come around.

"How did you know about my mother?"

"Never mind how I knew. How is she?"

"She's going to live, no thanks to you and…Who's responsible for what happened to her? Dr. Fischer or your husband?" It was not suppose to be like this. Sam had planned to cleverly trap Maria into a confession. Now Maria was in charge and Sam felt helpless.

Maria did not respond to Sam's accusation. Jessie had regained consciousness and was beginning to struggle to free herself from the bedpost.

"Sit still. You'll start bleeding again." Maria slapped her lightly on the face and then barked, "What are you doing here? Who told you to come here?"

"Dr. Fischer. He said I was to take care of Lisa."

Thirty-Nine

Samantha was right: Dr. Fischer's receptionist had come to kill her sister. Had she not been there, she would be dead by now. But, Sam, too, could have been killed.

Maria checked the ropes that bound Jessie to the bedpost and led Sam from the room. As they descended the stairs, Sam asked, "Where's my sister? What have you done with her?"

"She perfectly safe: she's with my husband. She's not ready yet. We'll bring her to you after we have explained."

"I thought your husband was dead?"

"So did the police. I tried to tell your detective he wasn't, but he wouldn't listen."

Downstairs, Samantha was guided into the living room and told to take a seat. Maria excused herself, saying she would return momentarily. Sam sat on the edge of a chair, then stood again and walked to the window.

What does she mean, she's not ready yet? She would demand an explanation the moment Maria returned.

But Maria was not alone. A tall, slender man with dark hair and brown eyes preceded her. With outstretched hand, he moved to the window and waited for Samantha to offer hers. "I'm Dr. Corelli, Miss Ballard. I regret we have never met before now."

Unable to raise her arm, Samantha stood frozen, her face ashen. She wanted to speak, but the words lumped in her throat.

Maria came to her rescue. She put her arm around her and eased her into a nearby chair. "We know, Samantha, how this must affect you. It has been hard on all of us, especially…"

Maria's explanation was interrupted by the ringing of the doorbell. Dr. Corelli opened the door. Detective Gordon stepped inside.

"Wes, thank heavens you've come!" Sam moved quickly to his side. "They have Cindy! She's here!"

The detective shot a glance of disbelief at Sam, then promptly focused on Maria and her husband. He had been convinced that the remains dug up from the woods were those of the kidnapped twin. He was still convinced.

The doctor extended his hand again: this time it was received by the detective. He introduced himself, then said, "The young lady is right: her twin sister is upstairs. She has been with us since the day we took her."

Samantha's knees buckled. Wes grabbed her moments before she reached the floor.

They lifted her onto the sofa and loosened her clothing; then the doctor continued. "She'll come around in a moment. The shock was too great for her."

"It's too great for me," Gordon admitted. "Confessions seem to be popular today. Are you sure you want to take this any further? Without an attorney, I mean."

"I'll call our attorney later. I'm sure Maria and I will be in need of his services eventually. Right now, I want to tell you a very long and pathetic story, and I think we need to do it without employing the law. Maria, would you bring coffee? I believe our young patient is beginning to come around."

Dr. Corelli waited until Samantha was fully alert and Maria had brought coffee. Sam and Wes remained seated on the sofa while Maria sat in the chair beside them. Corelli remained standing. The atmosphere was electric with anticipation; the doctor began.

"Maria came to me shortly after she was discharged by your father, Samantha. She was very much disturbed by…" The doctor searched for an appropriate word. "...by conditions at your home, but was bound by a promise to your mother to say nothing to anyone. The anxiety led her to me—as a patient. She knew I would be required to keep everything she told me confidential. Needless to say, I was most sympathetic with her dismay and urged her to lighten the burden she was carrying by returning to your mother for a release from the promise."

At this point, Wes was becoming impatient. He started to speak, to urge the doctor to be more explicit, but the doctor intercepted his comment with the wave of his hand.

"Please, bear with me, Lieutenant. I must lay the groundwork first." He sat in the matching chair opposite Maria and directed his gaze toward her. "Maria could not bring herself to return to Mrs. Ballard, but instead, returned to me in even greater distress. Our visits resulted in a social relationship and a few months later, I asked her to marry me. She accepted." The doctor smiled and continued. "This may have solved some of our problems..." He turned and looked at Sam. "...but the problem at your home remained, Samantha." Studying her response, Corelli waited.

Bewildered, she said, "I don't understand. What problem are you talking about?"

"You were young, I know, but were you truly unaware that there was a serious problem in your home?"

Sam paused, contemplating. "I...I was just a child. I...don't remember. My mother and father argued a lot, but I just assumed that was normal. I guess I ignored it."

Gordon was becoming uncomfortable. He was aware of the money Ballard was embezzling, but he was not sure this was what the doctor was referring to. He wasn't even sure if the doctor *knew* about the money. No, it was something else, something even more sordid, and Gordon wasn't sure if Samantha should hear it. He stood and asked to speak to the doctor privately.

The two walked into the doctor's office and closed the door. Gordon spoke first. "I have a hunch you're going to tell us something pretty disgusting, Doctor. I'm not sure how Sam will take it."

"Then you've found out."

"Let's not play games. It's incest, isn't it?"

The doctor nodded. "I suppose you see a lot of it nowadays."

"Too much. Was it just Cindy? Can we spare Samantha? Does she need to know?"

"As far as we know, it was only Cindy. But there's far more to the story than Ballard's abuse of his own daughter, and Samantha will never understand the rest without knowing everything. Trust me, Lieutenant. This is *my* field of expertise."

The detective did not respond immediately, but was beginning to sense he was dealing with a rational person, rather than a criminal. He was ready to gamble on him. "Okay, Doc, but there's something *you* should know before we go back in there. Ballard's dead. Fischer shot him."

"Yes, I know. He called me right after he did it. He wanted me to protect him. I told him to go jump in the lake. The man's crazy."

"Then you know about Carla."

"That he's been pumping Valium into her? That's my fault. I stopped seeing her regularly three months ago. Had I continued giving her the care she needed, I would have seen it and gotten her out of there. It was Nora that alerted me just yesterday."

"Nora?"

"The nurse. She said she gave you the lab reports."

"Hmm. No, it was more than the Valium. He tried to poison her last night. She almost died."

"I didn't know! Is she going to be okay? Where is she?"

"St. Vincent's. Sam was with her all morning. She's coming around."

The doctor sat down and supported his head in his hands.

"There's more," the detective continued. "Ballard was embezzling from the bank—thousands over the years. He and his girlfriend were ready to fly to Mexico City this morning, but Fischer wasted him first."

Corelli snorted. "Maria suspected something—something more than child abuse, but she didn't know he was taking money." The doctor shot up from the chair. "Then that's it: that's what Carla could never tell her. It's the one thing..."

Gordon placed his hand on Corelli's arm. "This is getting too complicated, too much for Sam, Doctor. It would devastate her. She thinks it's as simple as marital infidelity and she has accepted that. She doesn't even know her father's dead yet."

"You're right, all this is more than she should have to bear, but we have to take that chance."

"Why?"

"For Cindy's sake—and Carla's—and Maria's and mine."

"Then it's not entirely altruistic?"

"No, not entirely." The doctor opened the door. "Come. Trust me."

Forty

Upon returning to the living room, the two men found Samantha staring out the window. Dr. Corelli took her by the arm and led her back to the sofa. Wes sat beside her.

"Let's continue," said the doctor. "Samantha, I want you to prepare yourself for a very great shock. But you are strong; I know you can handle it."

Still wary of his motives, yet willing to listen, Sam straightened her posture as if to agree with his observation. "Go on, Doctor; I won't pass out again."

"I think at this point, I would like Maria to tell you what she discovered while she was working for your parents." The doctor turned to his wife. "Maria?"

The woman hesitated, uncertain as to what she was to reveal. She looked to her husband for an answer.

"Yes, dear, tell her. She has to know."

Maria shifted her attention to the twin. She cleared her throat and began. "Sam, do you remember the time you told me about finding your father at his desk in the middle of the night and how upset he got? He told you not to tell your mother, but you told me."

"Yes, I remember."

"And you later caught me trying to open his desk drawer."

"Yes."

"Well, I did succeed in getting the drawer open one day when you were in school. I found…" Maria looked again at her husband, not wanting to continue. He nodded. "I found magazines—pornographic magazines."

Sam was taken back, but was not yet ready to abandon her father. "Is that all? What's so bad about that?"

"The magazines were not simply pornographic, Sam. They were disgusting. They were of children."

Sam stiffened. "Children?"

"Yes, just like you."

It was difficult for Maria to go on, but she continued, gently leading to the revelation that she later found Mr. Ballard with Cindy. He was fondling her, sexually. She was six at the time.

Samantha remained silent, stunned. Maria continued.

"I went to your mother and told her. She denied it, of course. She could not bring herself to accuse him. A few months later, when Cindy was extremely upset and your mother couldn't calm her, I took her for a walk..."

Sam interrupted. "I remember. You wouldn't let me go with you."

"Yes. While we were walking, I got Cindy to admit that her father had touched her again—in her private parts. This time, your mother listened to me. The next day she kept you from school and we went to the beach."

Sam looked up, then at Wes.

Maria continued to tell the story of how she had begged Carla to confront her husband, but she was too frightened. "She told me she couldn't, that there was something else he had done. She said he had threatened to kill her if she ever told anyone. She wouldn't tell me what it was."

Samantha stood up. "I don't believe you! You are making this up! Then why did you take Cindy away? To protect her, I suppose! You're saying this to save your own skin!"

"No, Samantha, please believe me. This went on for three years! It reached the point where your mother couldn't handle it any longer; she was ready to crack!"

Wes stood and put his arm around the distraught girl. "Sam, whether it's true or not, we need to hear them out. Sit down. We'll find out later if they are lying."

The two sat again; Wes held her hand in his to comfort her.

Maria continued her story. "It was when you two girls were nine that your father fired me. I couldn't see your mother suffer any longer, and although I wasn't certain your father was still abusing Cindy, I had reason to believe he was. I went to him and accused him. He denied it, of course." Tears were beginning to form in Maria's eyes. "It was stupid of me to accuse him: I had no proof."

Dr. Corelli came to his wife's rescue. "That's where I fit into the story, Sam." He told her how she had come to him for advice and how they had eventually married. And how over the next three years, Maria had secretly stayed in touch with Carla, supporting her emotionally, until one day Carla decided she would leave her husband and take the girls with her.

"Your mother asked Maria to help her," Corelli said. "She said she couldn't ask him for a divorce: he had threatened to take her life if she ever left him or revealed to anyone something she still hadn't told Maria."

Wes knew the secret had to do with his embezzling money from the bank. By intimidating her, he was protecting himself from being caught. He could feel Sam's hand relax in his, the tension turning to trust. The incredible story they were hearing was beginning to sound believable. Either it was genuine, or the Corellis were excellent actors.

Maria picked up where her husband left off. "Your mother had a plan that sounded quite plausible. She had worked out every detail, and it seemed to be the only way she would ever get away from him. She wanted Tony and me to kidnap you two girls and to hide you for a month or two until the police gave up looking. In the meantime, she would fake depression and eventually just disappear, making it look like suicide. Then the three of you would fly to Brazil."

Samantha was captivated. The story was so incredible that she was unable to ask questions. Wes asked them for her.

"Then why did you take only Cindy?"

"Because Cindy was alone," answered Maria. "I was alone in the car and I just didn't use my head. The plan was for you to be with her, Sam." Maria reached over and took Samantha's hand into her own. "Tony was waiting for me in his car; everything was timed down to the minute. I just didn't know what to do!"

Samantha jerked. "Yes! I remember Mother tried to get me to go with Cindy. She kept urging me to go, but I wanted to stay and read my new book!" She turned to Wes. "I remember now, Wes!"

Gordon squeezed her hand and then turned to Maria. "The rental car, what happened?"

"It was after I picked up Cindy—she came with me willingly—I was driving on a narrow mountain road, a cutoff to get to McKinley's Market where I was to meet Tony."

"And where you were to pick up the money."

"That's right. We had to ask for ransom—to make it look like a real kidnapping. Besides, Carla and the girls would need the money later. She knew her husband had that much and more."

"Then you intended to take the money?"

"Of course, for Carla."

Gordon shifted the next question to the doctor. "Didn't you realize this would complicate matters? Had you been caught, the taking of the children might be explained. You could have told the courts the reason, and if the child abuse were proven, you might have got off. But the money, that's another matter."

Corelli waved his hand. "That's exactly what I told Maria when she came to me with Carla's unthinkable plan. But Carla had convinced Maria that he had the money and that technically everything was half hers anyway. How else would she get it?"

Wes continued. "Yes, and we know he had the money, don't we, Doctor?" The innuendo passed over both Maria's and Samantha's heads so he went on. "Let's get back to the rental car. It's my guess that you went over the embankment when a deer ran in front of you. Am I right?"

"That's what happened. It was the second flaw in the plan. I wasn't hurt, but Cindy was knocked out. I was able to get her out of the car before it caught fire. Tony was worried about us when we didn't arrive on schedule and came looking for us. I had just climbed back up and onto the road when the car burst into flames. Tony found us moments later."

Dr. Corelli took over. "I examined Cindy immediately. She had no apparent injuries, but remained unconscious for several hours. We brought her here, of course, and I watched her very closely."

"Why didn't you take her to a hospital?"

"There was a message on the recorder when we got home: it was from your mother. She begged us not to turn ourselves in and to keep Cindy with us. She said her husband would kill her if he found out the whole thing was her plan. And Maria felt certain he was capable of such an act. Carla didn't know Cindy had been hurt, of course. Later, she convinced us both that we had to remain out of the picture. But there were two things we didn't count on. When Cindy woke up, she had total amnesia of her past."

"And the second?" questioned Gordon.

"The second? It was Carla. She didn't have to fake the depression; she was truly consumed with guilt. The entire plan had failed and she couldn't cope with the results. The need for hospitalization and her husband's willingness to pay for it came as a blessing. Especially, since she still had the presence of mind to request admission to *Serenity*."

Wes realized at this point that Samantha was feeling very much forgotten. He turned to her and brushed the tears from her cheeks. "I think this is just about as much as this young lady can handle, Dr. Corelli. And I am going to have to take you two in. But if your story proves to be true, you shouldn't have to worry too much. In the meantime, what do we do with Cindy? I would like to meet her, if you don't mind."

"Of course, Lieutenant. I think it would be wise if we place her in her sister's hands until we can continue to care for her. Do you anticipate they will hold us long?"

"No, not long. I'll do my best to support you—if your story proves to be true."

Samantha spoke up. "I want my sister to know the truth. I want her to know I am her sister."

The doctor hesitated, and then with much conviction, said, "She has been prepared for this, but there is one thing she need never know."

Gordon picked up immediately. "That she was sexually abused by her father?"

"That's correct. There's no need to bring that out. And that's why I wanted to tell you the story before our confession became a matter of record. Will you go along with me on this, Lieutenant?"

Gordon hesitated. Concealing facts in a case could cost him his job. He weighed the matter carefully and answered, "I don't recall your ever mentioning anything about incest, Doctor. Do you, Samantha?"

Forty-One

There was still a number of unanswered questions in Gordon's mind, and Sam had not yet been told her father was dead, but he couldn't bring himself to traumatize her further. He was eager to meet Cindy, to see the two sisters together, but another matter had to be taken care of first. It was not pleasant, but the cop in him took precedent.

He stood and read the Corellis their rights. "I'm going to have a car come and pick you up. They'll be taking you to the precinct where you'll be held. Later, I will formally interview you on tape, but I don't want you to say a word to anyone until I'm there. Do you have an attorney?"

"Yes," answered Corelli.

"You'll be talking to him first. Keep in mind that whatever you say may eventually appear in all the newspapers, on television, everywhere."

"You're thinking of Cindy," Corelli said.

"No, you are. Every minute."

"But what excuse can I give? There has to be a reason for taking her."

Gordon looked at the bewildered twin, sitting on the sofa, still paralyzed by the story she had just heard. He realized she had to be told about the embezzlement. He sat again beside her. Taking her hand, he spoke softly. "Sam, there's one more thing you must know. Your father was involved in another criminal act that your mother knew about. He had been embezzling money from the bank for years. Apparently, your mother found out and to keep her quiet, he threatened her life."

Sam was limp from emotional exhaustion. Too overcome to respond, she slowly lifted her head and looked into Wes's eyes, waiting for him to continue.

Wes saw her again as a child. It was the same pitiful expression she had eleven years ago when he had to tell her they had not found her sister. He reached out for her and she melted in his arms. And sobbed.

The Corellis stood aside and allowed the girl to let her emotions flow. There were tears in their eyes as well. No one spoke for several minutes—until they were interrupted by a noise in the entry. It was Cindy. They had no idea how long she had been there.

Maria led Cindy into the living room. The next few moments were difficult as she attempted to explain. Not knowing how much Cindy had overheard, she stammered and then paused. Before she could speak again, Dr. Corelli came to her rescue. He put his arm around Cindy's shoulder and simply asked her how long she had been there.

"Only a few minutes. But long enough to know you were talking about this girl's father and that he had embezzled a lot of money." She looked at Sam. "I'm sorry for you. I wish I could help you..." Cindy was staring at her sister intensely. "Who are you? Why do I feel I have known you before?"

Sam had taken control of her emotions, wiped her eyes and stood firmly on her feet. She looked directly at her long lost twin sister and said, "Your real name is Cynthia Ballard. I am your twin sister."

Cindy stood frozen. She glanced at Maria, at Dr. Corelli and back again at Sam. She studied her face, put her hands to her mouth to stifle a gasp and hesitantly said, "I don't believe you." She turned to the doctor. "She's lying, isn't she, Uncle Tony?"

Dr. Corelli stepped forward and put his arm around her. "No, my dear. She is telling the truth."

It was the mole on Cindy's left hip that convinced her sister they were twins. Samantha told her exactly where it was and then, she showed Cindy the mole on her own thigh. "We are mirror twins, Cindy," she said. With that, Cindy could no longer deny their relationship.

Dr. Corelli and Maria explained that there had been an accident and that it was the cause of Cindy's amnesia. But Cindy couldn't understand why she was never told until now that she had a sister, an identical twin sister.

It was evident that Cindy had remained upstairs until just moments before she was discovered at the entry. Without revealing that she had been sexually molested by her father, Dr. Corelli told her the entire story. He used the embezzlement and the threats to her mother as the reason for the pseudo-kidnap plan. Cindy listened attentively, but she could not relate to the *Cindy* they were talking about: she remembered nothing of the past. It was as if she were being told about someone she never knew.

Gordon made a phone call to the precinct to ask for a patrol car. Maria remembered Jessie still tied to the bedpost upstairs and suggested he ask for two cars. Gordon was put on hold and Chief O'Malley came on the line. "Where on earth have you been? We've been trying to get you for three hours!"

Wes had turned his cell phone and pager off. He had not wanted interruptions. "Sorry, Chief, but I must have left my cell phone in the car. Didn't know."

"Well, get in here. Fischer has confessed, we've got the history on James Ballard you asked for—you're going to love it—and Mrs. Ballard is talking and asking for her doctor—Dr. Corelli! Now, shall I have Thornton take over, or are you still on the case?"

"I'm still on it, Chief," Gordon said. "And you can call the lab about the DNA. They'll have to come up with someone else. I've found Cindy Ballard and she's very much alive."

Forty-Two

Two patrol cars had been sent: one for the Corellis and one for Jessie. The woman was unaware that Fischer had been arrested and was eager to tell all she knew in order to save her own skin.

Before climbing into the car, the Corellis convinced Cindy that she should go with Samantha.

After the Corellis left with a police officer, Cindy returned to the house. It was difficult for her to think of Samantha as a sister, but she was eager to talk with her.

"I have to admit, I was startled when I first saw you, but I was drawn to you. That's why I threw the pillow at Jessie."

"We have so much to talk about, Cindy. May I call you Cindy? It's your real name, you know."

"It will take a while to get used to it, but, yes, you can call me Cindy."

She went on to tell Wes and Samantha about her eleven years with the Corellis and how they had filled her needs. They had been good to her and treated her like a daughter. She had never known any other family—not that she could remember.

Cindy went on with her story. "There were times, though, when I knew something was lacking," she said. "Sometimes I would get these strange feelings that I couldn't explain."

"It was probably me trying to communicate with you," Sam said. "I tried so often."

While Cindy was packing a suitcase with a few items of clothing, Wes led Samantha back into the living room. He knew she would have to be told about her father: there was no point in delaying it further.

"You've probably been wondering about your dad, Sam, and where he is."

"I'm not sure I care at this point. I wouldn't want to have to face him," she said.

"Well, that won't be necessary. The shot I heard, on Fischer's veranda: we thought it was Corelli. Sam, it was your father he killed. They found his body this morning."

The news was accepted as if he were talking about a total stranger.

"Sam, did you hear me? It was..."

"I heard you." Sam's demeanor was somber. She seemed to be cleansed of emotion, unable to react. "Perhaps it's just as well," she said.

Gordon questioned whether leaving her alone with Cindy at this time was prudent. He was about to suggest that they all take in a restaurant together, to give them both some time to adjust, when Cindy bounced down the stairs with a suitcase in her hand.

"I'm ready," she said on a cheerful note. "I'm ready to learn all about my family." She handed Gordon the suitcase and reached out to take Samantha's hand. "I've been thinking it over. Maybe having a sister wouldn't be so bad, especially an identical twin. We could play some wonderful tricks on Uncle Tony and Aunt Maria."

Sam smiled and burst out laughing. She grabbed her sister's hand and said, "You were always the one to come up with mischievous ideas. Looks like you haven't changed a bit."

Gordon relaxed. They would be just fine alone. And together.

He followed them to I-5 where they turned south. He headed north to the precinct.

O'Malley's nose was red again. "Gordon, you're going to put me in my grave. Come in and sit down. I want to know everything!"

"Chief, I've been up for thirty-six hours. Can it wait?"

"No it can't! What's this about finding Cindy Ballard? Where? Where did you find her?"

Gordon eased into the chair, closed his eyes and let his head fall back. "She's been with the Corellis the entire time. I'll write up the report tomorrow. For now, will you settle for this?"

The detective briefly summarized the story of James and Carla Ballard's rotten life together, and how the Corellis had stepped in to help implement a plan that boomeranged. But he never mentioned incest.

"Cindy is with Samantha," he said, "She doesn't remember her and may not ever. But Corelli says they can develop a relationship that can be just as binding as if they had never been separated. For now, can we leave it at that? Can I go home for an hour of sleep?"

"No!" shouted the chief. "We've got three people downstairs, two that need interrogating and one that needs to go to the hospital for sutures. How did you come across her? You haven't read Fischer's confession. Nor the one this Jessie woman gave us. She really blew his defense when we offered to cut a deal." He gave Gordon copies of the confessions, then said, "And you haven't read this." He handed the detective a printout that revealed Ballard's past offenses. Gordon read it, raised an eyebrow and dropped it on the floor.

"The guy was a jerk," the chief said. "Don't know how he ever..."

Gordon wasn't listening. His head had dropped and he was beginning to snore.

The chief stood, walked over to the inert body that was ready to fall from the chair, grabbed him by the shoulder and shook him back to life. "You want Thornton to drive you home?" he asked.

"No, I've still got work to do." He ambled out of the room, down the hall and to the elevator. The chief followed him until the elevator doors closed. Shaking his head, he returned to his office. "Welcome back, Gordon," he said. "Welcome back to the living—and the dead."

Before leaving the precinct, Gordon stopped at the interrogation room where the Corellis were waiting. Unanswered questions still troubled him.

Their attorney was there and he recorded their brief confession. Then, unofficially, they told him that they had devoted their lives to making a good home for Cindy and to caring for her mother at *Serenity*, the mother she would probably never know. They felt responsible for what had happened and were fearful of how James Ballard might have reacted were he to discover what they and his wife had done.

In time, Cindy was allowed the freedom to come and go as she pleased. They had not wanted to stifle her development. Occasionally, she would help out at the hospital, cooking and washing laundry. It gave her a job and a means of earning money of her own, and it kept her out of the mainstream of life where she might be recognized by someone. But she was never allowed on the second floor of the hospital or at the hospital at all when Mr. Ballard visited his wife.

Dr. Fischer knew exactly who she was. After all, he had been the one to pick up the rental car for the Corellis. This had been their mistake. It became the tool Fischer later used to insure his own safety when he began using *Serenity* to fleece wealthy widows and their families of their fortunes.

Gordon thanked the couple for the information, took care of paperwork and turned them over to an officer.

Jessie's confession revealed much that even the Corellis didn't know. James Ballard had made special arrangements with Dr. Fischer regarding his wife's care. Fischer was to see to it that she never recovered—and Ballard paid him handsomely for that assurance. Apparently, Ballard's undoing was his last decision to have Fischer put her to sleep permanently. The confession said Ballard paid him $200,000 for that final act. Gordon guessed he didn't want any loose ends before leaving with Melanie Taylor for Mexico City.

Gordon was curious as to how Jessie knew so much. He stopped at her holding room and asked.

"Dr. Fischer and I were lovers. He told me everything," she said in her familiar husky voice.

"Then why did you rat on him?" Gordon asked.

"He got caught."

Forty-Three

It was 7:45 PM when Gordon arrived home. Aguila was sitting there in his car waiting with pizza. The sun was just setting and the air was cool—too nice to go inside. Gordon put the top down and Aguila came over. He slid into the passenger's seat and they started on the pizza.

"Called you at the precinct, but they said you were tied up. I figured you'd be hungry," said the PI.

Gordon told him the whole story, then said, "You were right. You knew all along it was Ballard."

"No, I didn't," said Aguila. "I just didn't like the guy. You're the one that first suspected him."

"Yeah, but not like this," said Gordon. "I never knew he was such a scumbag. They ran a history on him. He was picked up once when he was in high school for joy riding. In college they pulled him in twice for theft and twice for rape. But they never proved it: he got off every time."

"Dung, that's what he is! How'd he ever win over a nice lady like Carla Ballard?" Aguila reached for another slice of pizza. "By the way, I hear she's talking."

"Yeah, she's coming out of it. Her doctor says she's going to be okay. She'll get the Corellis off."

"You think she'll recognize Samantha?"

"Most likely. Corelli says it'll come back to her as soon as the Valium's out of her system—and she finds out her husband's dead. She'll know she's safe."

"One question you haven't answered. Did you ever find out why the twenty-five hundred every month to Corelli's account?"

"Uh, huh. Carla was siphoning it off to the Corellis in advance so when the time was right, they could buy the plane tickets to Brazil for her. It was also meant to help pay for the twins' expenses while she was faking her depression."

"Where'd she get the money?"

"Part of it came from her diamond ring; she sold it to some kid that made payments. Ballard never knew; they were laying the plans months before the kidnapping." Gordon pulled a piece of pepperoni off his shirt and put it in his mouth.

"Did you ever take a look at the report I gave you on Fischer and Corelli?"

Gordon swallowed a bite whole. "Geeze, Juan, I forgot about it. What does it say?" He reached into the glove compartment and pulled it out.

"Not a whole lot, except for the credit report on Fischer. A couple of years ago he was ready to go belly up, but Ballard bailed him out and paid off his loan. He now carries the mortgage on the whole place."

Gordon sat up. "On *Serenity?*"

"That's right. Guess it belongs to Mrs. Ballard now." The two had a good laugh over the irony of the thing. Then Aguila turned serious again. "Wes, why don't you leave the force? Come join us: we could use another partner."

Wes picked up the last piece of pizza and took a bite. A purple finch flew down from the tree and landed on the hood of the car: it tilted its tiny head back and forth as it waited for its promised dinner. Gordon broke off a piece of the crust and tossed it to the little fellow. "You're late," he said. "We started without you." He laid his head back on the seat and closed his eyes. "No, Juan. Thanks for the offer, but Sam will want kids. You've gotta have a steady job when there's kids."

ശ ഌ